AFTERNOON DELIGHT

"Look!" Athena whispered in awe.

Dominic leaned closer to examine the butterfly on her shoulder. She smelled faintly of lavender.

"It must think I'm a flower. I look like a giant poppy."

Dominic gingerly reached out a finger to the butterfly. The velvet of the coquelicot spencer she wore over her white lawn dress was soft against the back of his hand. She did not move away from him. The butterfly stepped onto his finger and he brought it around to show her.

"Ohhh," she breathed out softly. She reached out a forefinger to the creature. Her fingers felt cool. The butterfly opened its brilliant wings and flitted off in a crazy dance. "Oh." She looked up at him in disappointment. "It's gone."

He stepped back and drew a breath. She smiled innocently up at him. "Well"—he cleared his throat—"we'd better go back."

"Perhaps so," she agreed reluctantly.

He did not offer her his arm on the way back, but she did not seem to notice. What had come over him? In another moment, he would have kissed her. . . .

Books by Catherine Blair

THE SCANDALOUS MISS DELANEY

THE HERO RETURNS

ATHENA's CONQUEST

Published by Zebra Books

ATHENA'S CONQUEST

Catherine Blair

ZEBRA BOOKS
KENSINGTON PUBLISHING CORP.
http://www.zebrabooks.com

ZEBRA BOOKS are published by

Kensington Publishing Corp.
850 Third Avenue
New York, NY 10022

All Kensington titles, imprints and distributed lines are available at special quantity discounts for bulk purchases for sales promotion, premiums, fund raising, educational or institutional use.

Special book excerpts or customized printings can also be created to fit specific needs. For details, write or phone the office of the Kensington Special Sales Manager: Kensington Publishing Corp., 850 Third Avenue, New York, NY, 10022. Attn. Special Sales Department. Phone: 1-800-221-2647.

Zebra and the Z logo Reg. U.S. Pat. & TM Off.

First Printing: March, 2001
10 9 8 7 6 5 4 3 2 1

Printed in the United States of America

Chapter One

"But you see, miss, women's minds were not made to grasp such things."

Athena longed to shake the man.

"It's the way of nature," the bookseller continued. "They are constitutionally inferior in understanding. A book like this would only bore you, if it did not cause your mind a good deal of harm."

She closed her eyes and drew a deep breath. "But surely it cannot matter to you what I choose to read. I am paying you the full price of the book."

His thick hand remained protectively over the substantial volume. "Now now"—he attempted a pacifying smile—"why would you want to worry your head about such weighty things?" He examined the book's title, *On Enclosure and the New Industrialization*, with distaste. "We have a nice selection of Ackerman's fashion plates and a lovely new novel out by Miss Burney. It's all about the intrigues of London society. I am certain that it would be more the kind of thing that you would enjoy.''

''I am sure that I would enjoy it. But right now I wish to buy this.'' She pushed a banknote toward him and waited with a tight, expectant smile.

His face sagged doubtfully. ''Why don't you give it to your papa? Then he can explain the interesting parts to you.''

She really *was* going to shake him in a moment.

''I think,'' said a voice behind her, ''that it is, indeed, not a good book for you.''

Athena whirled around. The tall, dark man behind her was unmistakably foreign. ''I thank you for your opinion,'' she replied coolly.

''See, the gentleman is right. Why don't you pick out something more appropriate.'' Mr. Waggoner's heavy face defied gravity for a moment as it heaved into an avuncular smile.

''I want this.'' She spoke between her teeth to keep her voice from rising.

''I think,'' the man behind her intruded again, ''that a bookseller must be like an apothecary. He must sell his customer what they wish to have, regardless of his opinion of the doctor's diagnosis or the patient's sickness. You must let her poison her mind if she wishes to do so.''

Both Athena and the bookseller regarded the foreigner with bemused expressions. What was this man going on about?

Mr. Waggoner shook his head. ''I can run my bookshop anyway I like, and I won't be selling dangerous books to a mere slip of a girl. It isn't moral.''

She felt her self-control slipping. ''Then I am afraid, sir, that you have lost my patronage.'' She shot him a look of what she hoped was icy hauteur and retrieved her banknote. She turned again to the man behind her. ''And

I wish you good day, sir." She would have liked to suggest he go to the devil.

"Infamous!" she exclaimed, as the door of the shop swung shut behind her. "Inferior mind, indeed." She gave her skirts an indignant shake and started up the street. Bath was more provincial than she had thought. She had hoped, when she came over from Ireland, that Bath would live up to it's reputation as a haven of intellectuals, political and literary circles, and education for women. It was bad enough to face the censure of a shopowner, but to have that arrogant gentleman agree with him!

She was well on her way up Milsom Street, muttering dire imprecations in every language she knew, when a voice stopped her in her tracks.

"Mademoiselle."

"Yes?" She drew herself up to her full height before she turned to face the man from the bookshop.

"You left something behind." He bowed and smiled, but there was something of a mischievious twinkle in his dark eyes.

"What?"

He placed a parcel wrapped in brown paper into her hands. There was no doubt what it was.

"You bought it for me?" She was stunned.

He shrugged carelessly. "Against my better judgment."

He might be handsome, and he might be a gentleman, but he was as patronizing as Mr. Waggoner. "You are very kind. But I don't believe that I can accept a gift from a stranger," she said with as much cool dignity as she could muster.

His smile was slow and feline. "But I would enjoy having a beautiful woman in debt to me."

She shoved the book back toward him. She knew very

well she was plain; it was ridiculous of him to pretend otherwise. "You are insolent, sir."

He had the temerity to laugh. "And I thought I was being chivalrous, procuring for you your book."

"It was kind of you," she acknowledged stiffly. He had not taken the volume when she offered it back. She should insist, but it weighed temptingly heavy in her hands.

"You will not enjoy it." His dark eyes were twinkling down at her again.

"I beg your pardon?"

"It is not a well-written book. I think you would enjoy Twedlow's *An Inquiry into the Industrialization of Textiles* better, if your interests run in that direction.

She stared at him for a moment. "Thank you," she said at last. Was he mocking her?

He bowed again. "It is nothing. I hope that your opinion of the book differs from mine. In the future, you may wish to try Stuart's Bookshop. He, I think, will allow you to poison your mind and tax your understanding with impunity."

Before she could assess for certain if he meant this comment facetiously, he was gone. She scowled after him and then scowled at the book. Then with a shrug, she unwrapped the parcel and began to read the book as she walked home.

"Mary!"

She staggered backward under the force of the embrace. "I think you must have made a mistake," she stammered as she disentangled herself. Had everyone gone mad today?

The complete stranger looked back at her with a stunned expression. "But, Mary!" she protested, "How impossible that you would not recognize me! I'm Sophia Well borne, from Miss Offrey's Academy. Have I possibly become so hagged?'' She laughed and pressed her hands to her cheeks with a droll expression of horror.

"I am Athena Montgomery. Not Mary. I'm afraid I am certain that I don't know you." She smiled apologetically.

The young woman's own smile collapsed. "Oh dear." She gasped. "How terrible. How embarrassing." She stepped forward and examined Athena with a closeness that made her draw back. "How terribly embarrassing," she repeated, her eyes wide with alarm. "You do look so very like Mary! How foolish I feel. My eyesight is not perfect, I'm afraid. Do, do forgive me accosting you like I did. I really did think . . ." She broke off in confusion.

Athena lay a soothing hand on the woman's arm. "Please think nothing more of it. I am quite flattered." She tucked her book under her arm with the intention of continuing up the street.

"Oh dear. And I was so happy with the prospect of having an acquaintance in Bath." The young woman looked down and pressed her lower lip between her teeth. "We have just come here today, and I swear I don't know a soul."

Athena hesitated, her awareness of the lateness of the hour warring with her sympathy. It should have taken only a moment to buy the book. "You know me," she said pragmatically. "We have just been introduced." She shook hands with the woman with mock gravity. "Miss Wellborne, I believe you said?"

"Yes. I can see very well now that you are not Mary, Miss Montgomery, but I am very happy indeed to make your acquaintance." She was jostled at that moment by a group of young men talking boisterously as they pushed by. "How very crowded it is here! I never thought that it would be so. I had thought that Bath was quite a sleepy town. Especially now, when the weather is so dreary. It is nothing like I thought it would be. We had such a terrible time finding lodgings. We have finally settled on a place in the Westgate Buildings. It is not very big, but as it is only my brother, our grandmother, and myself, it suits us very well.''

Athena followed Miss Wellborne's gaze up to the flat gray of the wintery sky. "There are quite a lot of people here this time of year. I was surprised myself when I first arrived.'' The two women fell in step together. Athena noticed that Miss Wellborne had a maid with her, and inwardly winced at the realization that she had walked out of the house without bringing Betty. Well, she had only thought to be a minute, and the maid was forever complaining at having to climb the hill home from the bookshop.

"How long have you been here?" Miss Wellborne asked.

"Two weeks. I like it very well. There are several quite fine bookshops and lending libraries." She begrudgingly made a mental note to take the Frenchman's suggestion and try Stuart's Bookshop. "My sister Cassiopeia says she finds it very flat, but I think she is rather enjoying herself, as she is so very popular at the assemblies.''

Miss Wellborne gave a little skip. "Oh, I would so much like to go to the assemblies. I must have Charles take me. I do so hope that we will see you there, Miss Montgomery, for you are my only friend in town now. I was feeling quite dejected just this morning, and now I am hoping that Charles's business will take quite some time. We had a relation leave us a little bit of property just north of here, and Charles must settle things with the solicitor. My grandmama is unwell and has come with us to take the waters." She stopped reluctantly at the corner. "Well, I must turn off here." She smiled. "Thank you so much for not being cross with me. It was terribly rude of me to barge into a conversation with you. I must write Mary and tell her that I have found her twin! You are so very alike—I feel as though we are quite good friends already. Do say we will meet at the assembly tonight. Good-bye!'' She waved cheerfully and set off down the street.

Athena smiled to herself. What a peculiar day it had been for meeting people! She reached the Crescent only slightly out of breath. The early March air was invigoratingly cold, and as she entered the town house, she saw the telltale red in her cheeks in the small hall mirror. Auntie Montie would be as cross as sticks if she heard she had been out.

"Missus is up," the butler announced gloomily.

"Oh dear, I had not intended to be so late." She removed her bonnet and attempted to smooth her wind-ruffled hair in the glass.

"Athena, thank heavens you are back!" Cassiopeia darted down the stairs. "Auntie is throwing quite a fit. Do go and soothe her. You know I only put her into the fidgets. I will take your bonnet. Just go in to her. I told her you were talking with Cook about dinner." Her sister ushered her up the stairs and into the darkened room where their aunt spent most of her days.

"Where's Athena?" a cracked voice demanded from within.

"She's here, Auntie," Cass called out as she gave Athena a push into the room. She rolled her eyes expressively at her sister from the safety of the hallway.

"There you are, gel. Where were you? Ah, you've been out haven't you? I can smell the outdoors on you. Gone downstairs to talk to Cook indeed." Auntie Montie narrowed both her eyes and her lips in disapproval.

"I only stepped out for a moment."

"Did you indeed, missy? Well you certainly took your time about it. I suppose you think that Bath was made for you to be parading about and going to shops for fusty old books instead of looking after me.''

"No indeed, ma'am. I only thought that while you were asleep, I might pick up something I had ordered.'' She calmly picked up the shawl that had fallen to the floor behind the invalid's couch and folded it.

"Well I do hope you remembered to take Betty with you this time. I swear I don't know what your mother was about with you children. Naming you all after silly Greek people for a start. Really, it is quite preposterous. I suppose we should thank the stars she hadn't more children, or I would have had to tell people I had a nephew named Jupiter or something equally ludicrous.''

"Jupiter is a Roman name. You mean Zeus," she corrected, automatically, thankful that the question regarding the maid did not seem to require an answer.

"Jupiter! Zeus! This is exactly what I mean!'' Auntie Montie warmed to the topic. "I don't know what my brother was thinking, marrying that bluestocking woman. Frightfully unladylike! I shudder to think of the shockingly inappropriate knowledge she has given you girls access to . . .''

"Shall I open the drapes? It is a rather nice day.'' She crossed the room and opened the heavy, straw-colored velvet curtains without waiting for an answer. "I think you should consider going out in your chair later. You know that Dr. Lightner will be annoyed to hear that you skipped your trip to the Pump Room this morning.''

"It was going to rain. I could feel it in my bones. My rheumatics always act up when it is going to rain.''

"But it didn't.'' Athena smiled.

"It isn't my fault if the weather doesn't behave like it ought,'' the old woman snapped. She turned her head from the window, but Athena caught a glimpse of the slight, upward twist to her mouth.

"Well, in any case, it is very fine now, if a little gray."

"I suppose you would know, since you were out," Auntie Montie said dryly. "You were sent here to take care of me, if you recall."

"But Cass was here if you had any needs." She stacked several plates and cups half full of cold tea on a tray and then rang for them to be taken away.

Her aunt gave a derisive snort. "That featherwit. She does nothing but chatter. The silly creature wanted to go to the assembly tonight."

"And she certainly shall go. I will chaperone her. She was sent here for a Season, if you recall."

Auntie Montie's thin lips compressed even more. "If your mother would get her nose out of a book, she would give that girl a proper Season in London. Your sister's a pretty thing, even if she does have no more sense than a rabbit. And with your mother's family connections . . ."

"Auntie, don't be ridiculous. You know very well that Cass would have had a London Season if Uncle Robert was not so busy right now."

"Well what good is having an uncle who is Foreign Minister and an aunt who is a patroness of Almack's, of all places, if they are not to give her a Season?" she demanded indignantly. "Your Uncle Castlereagh is back from that stupid Vienna Peace Conference, the war with France is over, and I simply cannot see what could be more important than getting that silly sister of yours married off, so that you can come and be my companion."

"Well," Athena drew out the word facetiously, "I suppose that there are some people who would consider maintaining peace with France more important."

"Castlereagh." The woman snorted. "When I think of the Season Emily Castlereagh could have given your sister—the creature would have been married off inside of two weeks! Though, I daresay Lady Castlereagh only said she would bring the girl out because she knew good and well that her sister-in-law would much rather be reading some fusty old Greek text than bringing out her own daughters.''

Athena shrugged slightly. "I am quite pleased with the entire arrangement. I never wanted to go to London in any case. Cass is disappointed of course, but I suspect that she will enjoy being here as well. It is not as though either of us has been far from Ireland, or even Londonderry before.'' She shot her aunt a wicked smile. "Besides, if Mama had done her duty and brought Cass out in London, I should have had to go with her to help chaperone, and then you should not have had me as a companion until the autumn at the very least.''

Her aunt made a low noise of disgust in her throat. "It is not as though you will be a very good companion to me if you are chaperoning your sister every night of the week. Why did that dratted girl have to be born a beauty? If she had been as plain as you, we should all be much happier.''

Athena laughed as she sat down in the wing chair beside the settee. "We shall never know,'' she replied serenely. "Now perhaps you would like me to read aloud to you until luncheon?''

"As long as it is not one of your tedious old books. I never met a girl with more dull taste in literature. Shouldn't you be clandestinely reading Byron or some such thing?''

"I have read him. I have even met him. Neither impressed me very much.'' She settled the skirts of her serviceable brown dress and reached for the book she had brought in with her.

"I swear, there is not a romantic bone in your body.'' Auntie Montie laughed her dry, hoarse laugh. "Well, good. I won't have you running off with the grocer's son like my last companion.''

It was strange that the impertinent Frenchman should suddenly leap to her mind. If not romantic, it *had* been chivalrous of him to procure the book for her. Even if he had been rather superior about it. ''I shall begin *Ivanhoe*. I think that it will be quite romantic enough to suit you,'' she replied with a gleam in her eyes.

''I won't like it,'' her aunt retorted with conviction as she arranged her wraps more comfortably about her.

Athena ignored her aunt's declaration and, in a low, clear voice, began to read aloud.

Chapter Two

"Free at last!" Cassiopeia sighed as the carriage rolled away from the house on the Crescent. "I don't know how you stand her, Athena. She is quite an old dragon. I feel as though I am in pigtails again every time she fixes me with one of those gorgon stares!"

"She is difficult at times," Athena agreed, smoothing her gloves meditatively.

Cass snorted. "Difficult. That is diplomatic in the extreme. I never thought she would let us out of the house. Do say you won't stay on as companion to her. You shall be positively stupified with boredom. I know you say you want to remain a spinster, but I just cannot understand why. What if you turned out like Auntie? If you continue on with her, I am quite certain that you will. Come and live with me when I am married."

"But what if this hypothetical husband should object?" She smiled.

"Pooh. I would not accept an offer from anyone who

would object to you living with us," her sister replied with a confident toss of her golden brown hair. "You will be much happier with us," she continued blithely. "I always think I will run screaming out of the house when Auntie starts on one of her tirades. Though I can certainly understand why she would detest having me around, for she never planned on having me stay with her. It would have been much more convenient if I could have had a Season in London. It really was rather awful of Uncle Robert to have so many other things to attend to. It isn't as though I would have been any trouble."

Athena hoped her look of amusement was somewhat shadowed in the carriage. "I think that with the Corn Bill riots, Uncle has quite enough on his mind."

Her sister shrugged negligently. "It is inconvenient to say the least. At least then Lady Castlereagh could have chaperoned. I have quite the distinct feeling that as a chaperone, you do not *do*."

"What do you mean?" Athena bristled.

"Well don't get all cross." Her sister leaned against her. "It is only that every time I speak with people and say that you are my chaperone, their eyebrows shoot up and they ask if you are not married."

"How ridiculous. I am not going to get married."

"Well, of course I know that. And I pointed out that many old maids chaperone younger sisters. But I believe that the common thinking is that you are not really old enough. Lady Battford said that you were not old enough to be on the shelf yet at all."

Cass took the ringlet of pale hair that fell artfully from her upswept coif and coiled it around her finger. "I believe the ends of my hairs are splitting." She examined them closely. "Too much use of the curling tongs, I suspect. I shall have to cut it all off one of these days. Do you think I should get one of those wonderful, fashionable short hair styles? I daresay Mama would have seven fits. For a bluestocking, she is terribly old-fashioned in her notions about hair styles. I never supposed—''

''I am four-and-twenty! How can I possibly not be old enough?'' Athena interrupted indignantly.

Cass looked up from her curl in surprise. ''I wouldn't know. I only heard it from several people that you were not. I tried to explain that you were an intellectual, and that Mama and Papa never really intended for you to come out, and that you yourself never meant to marry or anything like that, but they looked at me as though I was a bedlamite.''

''Such fustian!'' She scowled. ''As though I am not responsible enough to drive off the fortune hunters and keep you in line.''

Cassiopeia looked out the window as the carriage slowed to a stop. ''I know. I said the same thing. Good heavens, Athena, you look cross enough to be anyone's duenna. Please don't scare off all my beaux!'' She laughed as she allowed the footman to open the carriage door and hand her out.

Athena followed, gave her gown an irritated shake, and walked after her sister into the Upper Rooms.

''Good heavens, what a squeeze!'' Cassiopeia exclaimed.

''Well if you hadn't taken so long in getting dressed, we should have been here a good deal earlier.''

''Yes, but then no one would have been here,'' her sister replied with irrefutable logic. ''I see Celia over there by the fireplace. Do let's go over and say hello.''

They made their way slowly through the octagonal room, their progress severely impeded by her sister's numerous acquaintances.

''Celia! I declare, it took us quite half an hour to make our way over here. It really is a crush, isn't it? Good evening, Lady Beetling.'' Cassiopeia bowed gracefully to her friend's mother. ''You remember my sister Miss Athena Montgomery.''

''Of course.'' That lady replied, examining Athena thoroughly with her lorgnette. ''Miss Montgomery, there appears to be someone trying to attract your attention.'' She trained the glasses over Athena's shoulder and stared hard.

''Mine?'' Athena said in surprise. She turned to see who Lady Beetling was looking at. ''Why, it's the young lady I met on the way home from the bookstore this morning!'' She watched as that woman's blond head made erratic headway toward them as it bobbed about in the sea of people. She caught Athena's eye and waved enthusiastically.

''Hello, Miss Montgomery!'' She gasped as she emerged beside them at last. ''How glad I am to have found you. I never saw such a crush of people! I really thought I should expire on the way through. But here you are looking so cool and collected, just as though you were not in the middle of complete mayhem!'' She laughed. ''I daresay when the dancing begins it will only become worse.''

''Indeed there are far more people here than usual this Season. I suspect people are down from London because of the riots,'' Lady Beetling supplied. ''It is such a terrible time to be in town. I hear the mobs are breaking windows. I daresay if the Corn Laws pass, they shall burn the whole West End down.''

Miss Wellborne's slim white hand fluttered to her throat. ''I hear that it gets worse every night.''

''We shall all be murdered in our beds.'' Lady Beetling sighed with doleful satisfaction.

''Lady Beetling, this is Miss Sophia Wellborne,'' Athena interrupted their exchange of doomsaying. ''I met

Miss Wellborne just this morning.'' The two ladies bowed to each other.

"I have brought my brother with me.'' Miss Wellborne looked anxiously through the crowd. "There he is. I don't see how anyone could find anyone in such a mass of people.'' A handsome, rather serious-looking young man made his way toward them. "Charles, I have found Miss Montgomery at last. I told you that we should come upon her again. And she has introduced me to her friends. Now we shall have any number of acquaintances.''

Mr. Wellborne smiled and bowed over Athena's hand. "How very kind of you to have taken my sister under your wing.'' He looked rather like Sophia: fair and even-featured. Athena was reminded for a moment of the profile on a Roman coin.

"Indeed, it was nothing. She is so very charming,'' she replied, wondering how it was that she had taken his sister under her wing when she had only met the girl that morning. She turned to Lady Beetling. "Mr. and Miss Wellborne are here with their grandmother.''

"Indeed? Who is she?''

"Mrs. Joseph Wellborne,'' Mr. Wellborne replied. "We have only just arrived. I don't think that you would know her.''

Lady Beetling thought for a moment, her lorgnette trained on the ceiling. "No. I don't know her,'' she announced sadly at last.

"She is unfortunately very ill. She is quite bedridden and cannot leave the house. We are hoping that the waters may bring her relief.''

"We must hope so. This is my daughter Celia and Miss Montgomery's sister Miss Cassiopeia.'' She pulled her daughter by the elbow from a very giggly *tête-à-tête* with Cass. The girls tittered through the introduction and continued to roll expressive glances across the room.

Athena sidled up to her sister. "Whatever has come over you? You sound like a pair of schoolgirls," she admonished in an undertone.

"Do you see that man over there?" Cass indicated with a toss of her head.

Athena's eyes followed the direction her sister's unsubtle gesture. It was him! The Frenchman from the bookstore stood speaking with the Master of Ceremonies. As she watched in horror, he turned to look in their direction.

"What about him?" she asked, as her sister collapsed into another fit of giggles.

"It is said that he is a French spy."

"A spy? Good heavens, Cass! What a complete ninnyhammer you are. Where did you get such Gothic notions?" Athena recalled with a cringe how rude she had been to him.

"Celia has it from very good sources."

"Indeed. From her own head more likely."

"Well he is terrifingly handsome," Celia retorted, in her own defense.

"Then it makes perfect sense that he is a French spy," Athena replied with asperity.

"Everyone is saying so," Celia objected "And I do know he is French. I heard him at the Pump Room the other day. Look!" she squealed suddenly.

"He is coming this way!" Cass breathed. The two girls clung to each other, their suppressed squeaks sounding very much like two mewling kittens.

Athena watched in discomfort as the tall, dark-haired man crossed the room. The Master of Ceremonies was accompanying him. There was no doubt; he meant to ask for an introduction.

He walked past both Celia and Cass with only a glance of mild amusement. Athena dropped her gaze to the ground and waited for the inevitable. The two men passed her by without a glance and stopped in front of Sophia. Athena's head jerked up in surprise.

"I am Mr. King, Master of Ceremonies of the Upper Rooms," Mr. King announced unnecessarily. "Monsieur Solage has requested that I conduct an introduction between you." Mr. King was speaking to Sophia, but the Frenchman was looking at her. One of his eyelids dropped in a slow, conspiratorial wink. She was too stunned to respond.

"How do you do, Mr. King," Sophia replied, her blue eyes as big as plates. "I am Sophia Wellborne."

"I am Miss Wellborne's brother," Charles Wellborne added with a faint frown.

"Indeed. Mr. Wellborne. I would like to petition that you introduce me to your sister," Solage replied.

Athena heard her sister's faint admiring gasp behind her. "Cass," she said, turning on her. "I will not have you staring and making a spectacle over two people being introduced. You would think you had never seen someone from another country before."

"But I haven't," she protested.

"Well it isn't as though he has three heads." Thank heavens Monsieur Solage had the decency not to make it public that they had met before. It made no sense that she should feel an overwhelming sense of disappointment that he hadn't wished to be introduced. "There, I see Lord Aston approaching. Yes, see, he is bowing at you. Surely he is coming over to ask you to dance. There is no need for you to be gaping at other people."

"Indeed, I think he will ask," Cass replied, enraptured and entirely distracted from the drama of the French stranger. "I think he is quite in love with me," she added with all the naïveté of an unaffected beauty.

"Do refrain from asking him if he is." Athena laughed and waved her sister off into the minuet that Aston had duly requested. She turned back to Sophia, only to find that she, too, had been swept into the set. Solage made Sophia a low bow as they took their places on the floor. He looked at her as though she were the only woman in the room. Athena felt an uncomfortable, empty sensation in her stomach.

She turned from them and saw Sophia's brother standing beside her, scowling darkly. "What is the matter?" she asked in an undertone.

"I am not sure if I like that man," he replied, his eyes trained on the couple.

"Why not?"

"I don't know. There seems to be something very bold about him. Asking for an introduction and all that."

"Many people ask for an introduction through Mr. King." He certainly had a right to do whatever he wanted. Just because he had bought her a book did not mean he wished to continue the acquaintance. She watched the couple as they began the figures of the dance. For a pompous, overbearing kind of man, he certainly knew how to dress. There was a certain Continental dash to the cut of the fine black coat and cream brocade waistcoat. Though they were practically the uniform of the Upper Rooms, he retained a look of exotic foreignness. Little wonder the girls had been thrown into fits.

Wellborne's frown deepened. "I just don't like it above half," he replied at last.

"It is only a dance," she reminded him gently. After the scene in the bookstore, she could hardly have expected Solage to ask *her* to dance. She was foolish to have entertained the thought.

Mr. Wellborne's mouth quirked into a reluctant smile. "Yes it is. And I have been very remiss. Would you do me the honor of dancing, Miss Montgomery?"

"Oh dear no!" she exclaimed with a start. "I am only

here to chaperone my sister. I do not intend to dance.
Thank you all the same,'' she added belatedly.

''You are your sister's chaperone?'' he repeated, with
gratifying surprise in his voice.

Mrs. Beetling, who had been standing silently beside
them, cleared her throat meaningfully. ''Indeed, Miss
Montgomery, I should think that your mama would have
accompanied you herself.''

''Mama and Papa are busy writing a treatise together,''
she explained firmly. ''I am quite capable of chaperoning
my sister.''

She had not been raised to be romantic, she told herself
sternly. Cassiopeia was the family beauty. She herself
was the serious one, the clever one. She bit the inside of
her lip in annoyance. There was no point in being maudlin
over a silly country dance. Loneliness was a sentiment
of an undisciplined mind.

Chapter Three

"Did you not think Monsieur Solage the most romantic creature imaginable?" Cass sighed, casting herself onto a couch and gazing at the ceiling with a ludicrous expression of rapture.

"He seemed very well mannered," Athena replied, not looking up from her whitework.

"Merciful heavens, Athena, there are times when I think you must be made of stone. He is simply the most dashing man in the whole of Bath." She smiled dreamily. "And after Miss Wellborne, he danced with *me*. I truly thought I would die. I don't know how I kept from falling over. Really, even *you* would have been affected if you had heard the things he said to me."

"Indeed? What did he say?" She looked up with interest at last.

Her sister pursed her lips in thought for a moment. "I suppose only the usual type of things. How lovely I was. How fortunate he was to have danced with the two most

beautiful women in the room. Meaning your friend Miss
Wellborne of course. And she is excessively pretty. I
quite detest her,'' Cass added cheerfully. It took her a
moment to recollect her thoughts and refocus her misty
upward gaze. "It was the way he said them,'' she
explained, with another gusty sigh. "It's the accent.''

"I fail to see how a foreign accent and an incomplete
knowledge of English should make commonplaces sound
mysterious and romantic.''

"You wouldn't understand. Everyone else was quite
as affected as myself. Every female eye in the room was
upon Monsieur Solage. Why, he only danced with a few
of the ladies who were present. I am the envy of all the
girls in Bath.''

"Did he say he would call?''

Cass levered up to a sitting position on the couch, looking somewhat surprised. "Why . . . no . . . I am not certain
that he did.'' Her mouth turned down in disappointment.
"I mean, of course he sent over the usual sort of flowers
and inquiries after my health this morning, but I suppose
he did not actually say that he wished to call in person.''
She narrowed her eyes thoughtfully.

"Then I would not give him any more thought. You
have plenty of other beaux who are quite unexceptional.
Even if they only have accents from Gloucestershire and
Somerset,'' she added with a teasing smile.

There was a knock on the front door that made them
both start.

"Merciful heavens! Who would come calling? Auntie
Montie will be livid!'' Cass exclaimed. "You know she
doesn't take visitors.''

The sisters ran to the window and tried to see who was
on the doorstep.

"Mr. and Miss Wellborne are here,'' Auntie Montie's
butler announced. If he was at all surprised to see the

two young ladies kneeling in the window seat with their noses pressed to the window, his impassive face did not show it. "Shall I tell them that you are not at home to callers?" he suggested placidly, as he presented them with the Wellbornes' card on a silver salver.

"It is the Wellbornes," Cass affirmed unnecessarily after a glance at the card. "I suppose we should have discussed an at-home day with Auntie. Perhaps she will not mind us receiving the Wellbornes. It is not as though they are gentlemen callers."

"Well, one is obviously. But they are not calling to court you. Auntie never forbade social calls from female friends." Athena's brow creased briefly. "Show them up, Duncan. I will answer to Auntie for it."

"How kind of you to receive us," Sophia Wellborne exclaimed, releasing her brother's arm and going to shake hands with each of the sisters in turn. "We have heard that you live here with your aunt and do not often receive callers."

"Auntie is not very well," Athena explained.

"She has an illness that causes extreme crossness," Cass added impertinently. She was quelled with a dire look from her sister.

"How very trying for you both," Mr. Wellborne said with a smile. "Sophia and I find ourselves in similar circumstances. Our grandmother is so ill that she is quite bedridden."

"I have come to believe that everyone who comes to visit Bath has a diseased and unpleasant relative here." Cass shrugged. "Not that—well I am certain that your grandmama is not unpleasant," she added hastily with a blush.

"Indeed she is not unpleasant, but she cannot take visitors. We are fortunate to be able to get treatment for her while we conduct our business." Miss Wellborne accepted a seat beside Cass. "I hope you both had a pleasant time at the assembly last night?"

"I think that you and I had the best time of all!" she replied enthusiastically. "Is he not the most romantic figure you have ever set eyes on?"

Athena turned away from that conversation with a faint sigh. "Mr. Wellborne. How pleased I am to see that you at least are not overawed by the simple appearance of a foreigner." She smiled as she rang for tea.

Charles laughed and seated himself beside her. "Overawed, no. Eaten with jealousy, yes. As a staid old John Bull, I shall never be able to compete."

"You must not let it affect you. I am certain that women of sense will look for something more than a charming accent."

"Are you a woman of sense?"

"I think so."

"Then I am glad to hear it," he replied, his expression so serious that Athena was taken aback for a moment. She gave an uncomfortable laugh and looked anxiously for the tea tray to arrive. "I do hope you are enjoying Bath," she said, realizing at once how inane she sounded.

"Indeed. In fact, Sophia and I came here with the express purpose of inviting you and Miss Cassiopeia on a picnic expedition to Farley Castle."

"How very kind of you to think of us," Athena replied. "I am not certain, however, that we will be able to accept." The tea tray arrived at last, and she began to pour out. "If there are others going, Cass would be happy to go, I am sure."

"And not yourself?" he asked in surprise.

"While I am here to see that Cassiopeia has a Season, I am also acting as a companion to my aunt. I am quite torn between my obligations, you see. But as long as there are proper chaperones for the picnic, I see no reason why I should need to go.''

His brows drew together in a disappointed frown. ''But we very much wish for you to go too. I must say, Miss Montgomery, I cannot understand why you are acting as either companion or chaperone.''

''Why not?''

''Because you are far too young and pretty to be thinking of anything but pleasure.''

Athena stared into the amber depths of her tea, its heat increasing the flush she felt on her cheeks. She was not pretty, and she knew it. How irritating of him to have embarrassed her so, when he must have known that she would not know how to respond. It was, perhaps, nice to have heard the words though.

''I must apologize, Miss Montgomery. I have offended you. I only meant that Sophia and I would very much like for you both to come, if that is possible.''

''I will speak with my aunt. Who else will go?'' She was grateful he had let the awkward moment slip by.

Charles shifted. ''I am afraid the notion of chaperones had not entered our heads. We are from such a small town in Yorkshire that everyone knows everyone, and it is never an issue. My grandmother cannot, of course. We shall come up with something. I never realized how very stuffy everyone is about such things.'' He laughed easily.

''That is true. I am sure that Cass and I are the subject of all kinds of speculation. I am not considered at all old enough to be an appropriate escort.''

''I have already expressed my opinion on that head,'' he replied, with a wry laugh.

She felt the flush return. ''Indeed''—she forced herself to smile—''I am certain that we shall find someone to go with Cass, and Auntie will be pleased to have me to herself for the afternoon.''

"But do say that you will try to come yourself. Sophia counts on it. She feels so grateful that you showed her such kindness when she first arrived."

She made a dismissive gesture. "I am sure I only did what anyone would have done."

"Athena! Did Mr. Wellborne tell you? We are going to picnic to Farley Castle tomorrow. It shall be a real expedition! Won't that be great fun?" Cass squealed in enthusiasm.

"Yes, but do not set your heart upon it. You know Auntie Montie is likely to say no."

"Oh no! Don't say that! You will be able to talk her into it! Please say that we will go!"

"We will see," Athena said repressively, darting her sister an expression that begged her to let the subject drop.

Cass glowered, but remained silent.

"We will take our leave now. We only meant to stay for a moment and issue our invitation. Do try to come, both of you. We are so looking forward to it. Charles has hired a landau for the occasion." Miss Wellborne gathered up her belongings. "I hear your auntie ringing, so we will scamper away. I do hope that we have not set your entire household on ear with our visit and our invitation!" She laughed merrily as she began to gather up her belongings.

"It took you long enough," Auntie Montie said acidly as Athena entered the room.

"I am sorry. We had visitors." She took up the shawl, which always made its way to the floor when the woman was in a tiff, and folded it neatly.

"So Duncan said. I suppose you think you are mistress of the house now?"

"Not at all," Athena replied, seating herself to prepare for the tirade.

The old woman looked annoyed at this brief response. "I do not like having visitors. I will not have this house made into a circus full of floppy-haired poets languishing for your sister."

"But you *do* wish for her to get married?"

"Of course," she snapped. "The sooner we are rid of her, the sooner you can act like a proper companion to me."

"Then you must allow some callers. Mr. Wellborne is quite respectable."

"Hmph. Where is he from?"

"He and his sister are from Yorkshire, I believe," she replied, repressing her irritation.

"Where exactly?"

"I don't know, ma'am."

"Well you should find out. Your father's and my family is from there. Respectable people, the Montgomerys. Not like those Irish Castlereaghs. They're all mad as hatters but twice as dull. Bluestockings and literary men, every one. Lord Castlereagh's the only one who got anywhere and that's because he's a Tory. I know the rest of your family has Whiggish tendencies that have corrupted my brother. If my mother knew poor John had turned Whig . . ." The ribbons on her cap quivered with the violence of her inexpressible indignation. "Bookish, Whiggish, Castlereaghs," she spat out. "It was a wonder they ever got their noses out of their books to ever breed at all."

"I believe we were discussing the Wellbornes," Athena interrupted.

"Yes. Write your mama and ask about them. I'll bet she knows someone of their family if I don't. The county's littered with your relations. You can find out if these are respectable people.''

''Of course they are!'' Athena replied indignantly.

''Hmph. Always better to know something about these people. Wouldn't want your sister to marry the wrong sort.''

''I hardly think it has come to that.''

''Well if he ain't going to marry her, don't let him in the house.'' The old woman poked her finger at her niece. ''Besides. I've never heard of this grandmama of theirs.''

''How do you know anything about them?'' she exclaimed in surprise.

Auntie Montie lay a finger beside her nose and looked sly. ''Don't think that because I am rotting away up here I don't know everything.''

Athena rolled her eyes. ''Shall I read to you?'' she asked in exasperation. Poor Auntie liked to pretend she was irascibly fierce, but she loved a good gossip.

''No. I'm sick of that book. Tell me how soon we are likely to get rid of that sister of yours.''

''Cass will marry when she falls in love,'' she said firmly.

''Well don't let her marry that damn Frenchman she danced with last night. He's more than likely a spy.''

''Auntie! *You* are the spy!'' Athena burst into uninhibited laughter. She controlled herself with an effort, took up the book by the chair, and resolutely began reading aloud, oblivious to the loud protestations of her aunt.

Dominic Solage stepped down from the post chaise and stretched his legs. The weekly trip to London seemed longer every time. Ah well, it wasn't as though he was missing anything in Bath. A more staid, old matron of a city he had never seen. But the Bath water was the only thing that seemed to help Lord Falk's gout, so as long as he was the man's courier, the weekly journey would remain a necessity.

He waved away an offer of a sedan chair and began the walk up to the house on Rivers Street. At least this trip had yielded some interesting results. Falk's people in the Ministry of Commerce were deep into an investigation of various shipping company frauds. Several had been going on for years, neglected during the fervor of the war. Now that the peace treaty was signed, the schemes could be properly scrutinized.

He turned up the collar of his many-caped greatcoat. Across the street, a woman and her two daughters stared blatantly at him as they whispered behind their hands. He doffed his hat and smiled pleasantly at them. *Diantre,* but it was irritating. The ridiculous rumors going around seemed to have increased his consequence rather than otherwise. He had received sheaves of invitations since he had arrived. In London, he was invisible. Here he seemed to be the newest fashion.

"Well, how was the trip?" Falk's voice demanded from the library as soon as he entered the hallway. "Any news on the imaginary Portsmouth Shipping Company? What about the Jamaica Isles scheme?"

"You must allow me to take off my coat, sir."

"Botheration with the coat. Sit down and have a drink. It will warm you up."

Solage left his coat with the butler and went into the library. "Sir, you know that brandy—"

"Shut your mouth. I know good and well spirits ain't good for the gout. What's the news?" Falk poured a tumbler of brandy and then leaned over in his chair to stoke the fire to a blaze.

Dominic took a sip. "French brandy. For a government

man, you do seem to be able to acquire the best of the contraband.'' He grinned.

"Cut line, Solage. The war is over. Commerce is king now. We'll be trading all over the world before the cat can lick her whiskers, and Whitehall hired you to help me souse out the wheat from the chaff as far as new shipping companies are concerned. What did Rundall say about the Portsmouth Shipping Company? There's some chaff if I ever saw it. I'll lay a monkey those ships never existed.''

Dominic inched his chair further from the fire. Falk kept the place like an inferno. Heat seemed to be an English obsession. "While nothing has been discovered regarding the Portsmouth Company, it appears that the deWit brothers, of the Jamaica Isles scheme, have been traced here.''

"Here? Bath?'' Falk looked delighted. "How very polite of them to come to me. I shall be able to investigate the whereabouts of the dogs without leaving the comfort of my drawing room.''

Dominic closed his eyes and smiled with resignation. Of course he knew what was coming next. His host couldn't leave the comforts of his drawing room if he wanted to. With his gouty leg, Falk would play the role of director, while he himself would be the one to do the investigating.

"Get out there and put your ear to the ground.'' Falk gestured so enthusiastically that his brandy sloshed dangerously in its tumbler. "Go to all the parties those damn town tabbies invite you to. Dance with all the pretty girls. You should enjoy that part. The deWits will turn up somewhere. Bath can't keep a secret for the life of it. You'll hear something and we'll nab 'em.'' His host leaned back in his chair with an expression of satisfaction.

He thought of last week's insipid company at the Upper

Rooms. Even the prettiest girls had been uninteresting. Everyone stared and tittered behind their fans as though he were an exhibit from the London zoo. A spy indeed. He scowled and got to his feet. The only person in the whole place with any sense was Miss Athena Montgomery. He had found out her name when he was dancing with her sister. Perhaps she had too much sense. Any young lady who wished to read politics and could swear in four languages was a good deal too prim to indulge in the current gossip. He had had the urge to ask her to dance, but she did not strike him as the kind of young lady who might know the current *on-dits* regarding mysterious men in a shipping scheme. She wasn't anything beautiful, but there was something intriguing about her direct, gray-eyed gaze.

"Now," said Falk, "on to more important things. How's Castlereagh?"

"Very well. He sends his best wishes as to your health." Dominic pulled out a large bundle of papers from his satchel. "Here are a few of the things about which he wishes your opinion."

Falk's brows shot up. "That man is trying to kill me. When will he learn that it is time for me to retire and for you to take my place?"

"In his own time." Solage sorted quickly through the papers. "For now I shall continue to play the role of courier and advisor." He put any thoughts of clever young women with remarkable gray eyes out of his mind and turned to business.

Chapter Four

"I am going to nip out to Stuart's Bookshop. Do you wish to come with me?" Athena asked her sister as she buttoned her coal gray pelisse up to her chin.

Cass lay down her embroidery. "I suppose I will. I feel like I haven't been out of the house since the assembly, and that was days ago! I'm bored to flinders. But I will only go if you will not wear that thing."

"What thing?"

"That horrid pelisse. Why must you always dress like . . . like Mama?"

"What do you mean?"

"You look like the veriest bluestocking."

Athena regarded her sister in surprise. "I suppose it is because I am one."

"Well, yes, I know you are very clever, but really, Athena, I think that you deliberately make yourself unattractive."

"That is untrue. I am just uninterested in fashion."

She examined the pelisse as though for the first time. It was good quality and in reasonable condition. Perhaps the color was not the most flattering, but still . . .

"Do you know what I think? I think that you make yourself look plain so that you will not have to deal with the attention of men. You have lovely eyes, really, and your hair could be quite passable if you would only let Betty dress it with a bit more dash. You are a coward."

"Nonsense," she replied briskly, "I just do not wish to show you up, you vain little creature. Now are you coming with me or not?"

"Wait a moment and I will get my bonnet. I know, I will get my second best bonnet too. The one trimmed in red. You will wear that one. It will quite improve that horse blanket."

"Don't, Cass. I am quite happy as a duckling, you know. There is no need to dress me up in swansdown," she replied. But her sister had already disappeared up the stairs.

Athena felt somewhat foolish walking down Bond Street, wearing her sister's excruciatingly fashionable high-crowned bonnet trimmed in crimson. It made the dull, gray pelisse look even more unappealing. But Cassiopeia was happy; she pronounced the effect quite good and chattered away like a pot on the boil all the way to the bookshop.

"Oh do say you will!"

"Will what?" she asked blankly. She had been wondering what it was about the Continental cut of a coat that put silly girls into a tizzy.

"Have you been listening to nothing I have said? The expedition to Farley Castle! Do say that you will convince Auntie Montie to let us both go."

"I don't know. I am not at all convinced that it is quite the thing."

"Feh! You sound more like the old dragon herself every day. There will be enough of us there that surely no one will question the propriety of us going. Besides"— she smiled brightly—"you will be there, and if Mama thinks you are a good-enough chaperone for me, so should everyone else."

Athena was beginning to form the opinion that perhaps her mother's notions of propriety did not quite follow convention, but she kept this notion to herself. They entered the bookshop, and she inhaled deeply. Bookshops always had such a good, solid, reassuring smell. There. Who needed a pretty nose or poetry from a bevy of coxcombs like Cass had, when one could have this? She nodded a greeting to Mr. Stuart and then began a slow perusal of the shelves. The tension in her nerves slackened slowly as she continued down the familiar aisle. Cass trailed along after her impatiently.

"What are you looking for?"

"I don't know. I am waiting to see what appeals to me."

Her sister rolled her eyes. "But you are here every week. You know exactly the books that are here."

"Sometimes new ones come in," she retorted. "Besides, even though I know what is available, it is a wonderful feeling to know that I could possess any of them."

Cass made a dismissive noise.

"Like you," she continued, allowing her fingers a lingering caress of *Tom Jones*'s spine. "You know just what men always turn up at the assemblies, but isn't it nice to ponder which one you will pick?"

"I suppose that is true," her sister replied thoughtfully, oblivious to Athena's teasing tone. "Anyway, I am unlikely to meet any of my beaux here. I shall be quizzed

mercilessly for a bluestocking if I am seen by anyone."
She laughed good-humoredly. "Perhaps I can find a book
or pamphlet on growing herbs indoors. Mama's were
doing so poorly. I keep telling her to have Papa build her
a hothouse, but of course you know they will never do
it." She wandered toward a shelf of books labeled "Agri-
culture and Horticulture" with a pasteboard card.

Athena searched the shelves for a few moments. "Ah
there you are, my dear," she exclaimed softly, crouching
down to remove a slim leather-bound copy of Beckford's
Vathek. "I have been looking everywhere for you."

She had opened the book and begun to read in the aisle
when a quiet laugh made her look up in surprise.

"I feel as though I am listening to the reunion of lovers
who meet secretly in the night," said the unmistakable
voice of Monsieur Solage. He appeared around the corner
of the shelf.

"I have seen this book every time I am here, and I
have wanted to buy it for a long time. Today I decided
to get it, but I thought for a moment that I was too late
and someone had stolen it from me." She clasped the
book possessively to her. Why did he always seem to
catch her when she was doing something foolish?

"No book could be so untrue to someone like you,
Miss Montgomery." He gave a slight, courtly bow.

How did he even know her name? She decided to ignore
his comment; it would not do to encourage his boldness.
"Did you enjoy the assembly last night?"

He shrugged dismissively. "The more important question is: Are you enjoying your book? Not this one, the
banned one on enclosure and the, what was it? The new
industrialization?"

He said the title in such a comical tone that she could
not help but laugh. "I am not enjoying it, I'm sorry to

say. You were entirely correct. It is neither well-written nor well-informed.''

His eyes were teasing and warm. ''Then I am sorry I did not side with Mr. Waggoner.''

''You were very kind the other day. Both for procuring the book for me, and for not mentioning the incident at the assembly.'' Perhaps he was not so arrogant after all. She could certainly see how Cass and Sophia found him irresistibly charming.

He gracefully waved away her thanks. ''What book is it that you are so passionable about?'' he asked, turning his head to see the title. ''Ah, Beckford. You have a weakness for French literature, I see.''

''Indeed no, that is, I—'' She found herself inexplicably wishing for a moment that she had been born with Cass's beauty and inherent knowledge of light witticisms sparkling with double entendres.

''An Englishman, Beckford, but of course his best work was done in French,'' he said. She couldn't help but notice that he had very even white teeth when he smiled. ''I see that this volume is untranslated. You read French?''

''I do. Most Englishwomen do.'' She knew she sounded defensive, but it was too late. There was something about the man that made her feel . . . uncomfortable.

''Of course. But I think that most do not read it so well as to read this. Certainly not to understand its subtleties. Most only know the words of the fashions and the occasional phrases like . . . double entendre.''

Athena gave a start and laughed. ''I suppose that is true enough. My parents are both linguists. I was taught French at a very early age.''

''And Beckford, you enjoy his work?''

''Yes.'' Athena glanced down at the book she held and gave its cover a caress. ''I have read Henley's English translation, but I was curious to read Beckford's work in the original French.''

''Ah yes, published in Lausanne. While it is more representative of the author's work, it is lacking Henley's notes. Those are what the English seem to find most . . . edifying.'' One side of his mouth crept into a mocking smile.

''Yes, I suppose you might think that the English are unable to appreciate a story for its own literary merit without 'edifying notes.' ''

''There is no need to become offended, my dear Miss Montgomery.'' His dark eyes had that irrepressible twinkle. ''I did not mean you personally. You are said to be very well-read indeed. I am interested to hear your opinion of the work.''

Who had told him that she was well-read? Well, it was probably the most complimentary thing anyone could say about her. ''Indeed, I have developed quite an interest in the English representation of 'Oriental literature,' '' she said. ''I am sorry that I do not read Arabic, for it would be fascinating to compare the recent slew of Oriental tales with original texts.'' She noted in surprise that, instead of glazing over, his expression sharpened with interest.

''Then you do not ascribe to the notion that these are translations of original Arabic stories?''

''No. My aunt and uncle know Beckford quite well. The Castlereaghs used to see him often before he went to the Continent. The story is definitely from his own mind.''

''Castlereagh?'' he repeated, surprised. ''Lord Castlereagh is your uncle?''

''Yes, do you know him?''

''I—''

''Monsieur Solage! How very nice to see you again!'' Cassiopeia's bright voice made them both start. ''Athena, how very cruel of you to keep him all to yourself." The glance she slanted from under her lashes had proven fatal to the sheaves of admirers who had fallen before it.

"Ah, the charming Miss Cassiopeia Montgomery." Monsieur Solage bowed over her hand with perfect aplomb. "How fortunate I am today. I have found myself in the company of the two most lovely ladies in Bath."

Athena stifled the urge to roll her eyes. Just when he had started to seem interesting, he revealed himself as just another vapid coxcomb.

Cass giggled. "How you do run on." She pretended to scowl and rapped him in on the arm with her parasol handle. "You shall make us so vain that we shall never get any beaux. We shall be quite spoilt, and it will be your fault."

"Miss Cassiopeia, I think that you are like the strawberry preserves. You are too sweet to ever spoil."

Athena covered a sarcastic snort with a cough. The resulting noise was somewhat alarming.

Her sister's mouth turned down in a pretty moue. "Monsieur Solage! Any more of your outrageous compliments, and I will fall quite in love with you." She rapped him again with the parasol handle. "I do not wish to be another victim of your charm. I'm sure half of France must have gone into a decline when you left the country."

"A decline?" he said blankly.

"Death from boredom," Athena translated cynically. "Cass, I must make my purchases, and then we will go. We have been here far too long, and you know Auntie wished to go out in her chair this afternoon."

"But you must allow me to accompany you home," the Frenchman insisted.

"That is not at all necessary," she replied, before Cass could get a word in. "We do not live very far away." She felt the parasol handle jab her in the back.

"Oh, but mademoiselle, I will do so for entirely selfish reasons. Think of how it will increase my consequence to be seen with not one, but both lovely Montgomery sisters."

Athena smiled thinly and turned to go to the front counter. How irritating. It was one thing to do the pretty and quite another to lie to an extent that it was insulting. For two minutes there, he had seemed like a rational, educated man. She shot him a darkling glance. Cass was laughing delightedly and had begun to wield her parasol with even more flirtatious vigor. Solage looked up and returned her gaze, his expression inscrutable. Once they were outside, Monsieur Solage stopped them both.

"First I must disarm Miss Cassiopeia," he said, taking the parasol from her with a bow. He opened the sunshade and held it over her sister. "And then I will take the book from the most grievously insulted Miss Montgomery." He took the package from Athena's hands and then offered her his arm.

"On the contrary, Monsieur Solage, I am not insulted," she was forced to say.

"Athena is just serious," Cass volunteered.

"Indeed," he replied, chastised. But Athena saw a definite gleam in his dark eyes as he inclined his head to her. She clenched her teeth. How dare he mock her! She wasn't the one making a fool of herself with ridiculous compliments. She would rather be ignored than flattered with praise that was patently untrue.

She watched him critically as he continued to banter with Cass. He was excruciatingly handsome, it was true. If one was the type who admired classically dark. Perhaps his nose was a little too aquiline and his brow too broad. His eyes were undeniably fine, embellished with dark lashes and a black slash of eyebrow. But they definitely showed a tendency toward a poetic brooding that she herself found tiresome. Even if they did flash with good humor on occasion, certainly his extravagant flirting could not be considered in the best taste.

By the time they neared home, Cass's incessant laugh had begun to give her the headache.

"Oh, Athena, I just had the most marvelous idea!"

"What is it?"

"We will ask Monsieur Solage to accompany us on the expedition to Farley Castle! It will be a grand party. Isn't that a lovely idea?"

There was no way to uninvite him now. "I am sure that it would be very pleasant. However, we are not certain if we will be able to go on the picnic ourselves, if you remember."

"But you will talk Auntie into it. I am certain that you can talk her into anything." Cass gave a skip. "Do say that you will come, Monsieur Solage. The weather has been so pleasant lately that it is bound to be a fine day. I declare, I am quite ready for it to be spring."

"I am unsure what the Wellbornes were thinking when they conceived this trip. The weather is so very unpredictable this time of year." Athena grumbled.

"Don't be a wet blanket! We shall have a marvelous time." She stopped in front of the door and impertinently held out her hand for the Frenchman to kiss. "I am depending on you to come with us."

"I shall do everything possible."

"Thank you for accompanying us. It was very thoughtful," Athena interposed dampeningly, one foot on the steps of the house.

He captured her own hand and bowed over it. "It gave me great pleasure." His eyes were laughing at her again.

"Monsieur Solage, may I have my parasol back?" Cass demanded with a dimpled smile.

He turned back to her sister. "I think that I might keep it."

"How foolish you would look, walking down the street with my silly yellow parasol!"

"No, I will keep it as the collateral, so that I will be assured of seeing you again. You are very fond of the silly yellow parasol, no?" He closed it carefully and tucked it possessively under his arm.

"Do stop this nonsense. Auntie will be livid that we have been out so long," Athena snapped.

Cassiopeia looked at her in surprise. She retrieved the parasol with reluctance and followed her sister into the house.

"Whatever made you behave so horridly?" she demanded, once they were within the door. "Monsieur Solage will think that you are quite an old shrew."

Athena scowled. "I'm sorry Cass. I . . . I was just . . . it seems that he is so very insincere. I do hope that you do not believe everything he says. I am convinced that he is only doing the pretty. In a very excessive way of course, but perhaps that is just the French mannerisms." There was no sense in venting her spleen to her sister. Besides, the charmingly insincere Monsieur Solage would likely bow out of the expedition when something more appealing arose.

"Of course I do not take him too seriously." Cass looked insulted. "I am no green girl! But I do think that he has shown a definite interest in me, and he is quite the most eligible man in Bath. I will not have you ruin it by being rude to him. It is very unlike you, Athena."

She pursed her lips and drew a breath to calm herself. "I know. I just have the headache, that is all. Continue with your flirtation with him, only don't let him pull the wool over your eyes. We know nothing about him."

Her sister rolled her eyes. "I am certain he is not a

fortune hunter, if that is what you mean. He is staying here in Bath with his godfather, Lord Falk. You cannot ask for more respectability than that. Solage is well set up indeed. There is no fear that he is after my fortune. There now dear''—she patted Athena's hand—''go and lie down with your headache. I am glad it is only that. For a moment I thought that you were jealous, and I would have felt terrible. You know how much I admire you, you being the clever one and all. I am quite the disappointment of the family since I have only my looks and no cleverness.'' Cass looked sincerely dejected for a moment.

''Do go upstairs,'' she continued sympathetically. ''I will ask Cook to send up a tisane. But, Athena''—she stopped her sister who was ascending the stairs—''could you look in on Auntie first and convince her to let us go on the picnic?'' She gave her a wheedling look and then disappeared in the direction of the kitchen.

''I don't know how I got the reputation of the clever one,'' Athena muttered as she headed toward her aunt's room, ''when I am obviously an idiot.''

Chapter Five

"I don't know how you did it," Cass marveled in a low voice as the landau rolled down the Bristol road.

"To be honest, I am not certain how it came about either," Athena replied. "Of course it was touch-and-go even as late as this morning. But when the weather turned out so fine, she said she would accompany us." They both watched Auntie Montie's old-fashioned bonnet bob in response to something Monsieur Solage was saying as he rode beside the carriage on his black horse.

"Amazing," Cass breathed. "I believe she has taken quite a shine to Monsieur Solage. How marvelous! I do hope that means we will see more of him."

"I suppose he could charm the leaves off a tree if he had a mind to." Athena smoothed her gloves and frowned. "Anyway, it has solved the problem of a chaperone quite nicely, so I will not complain. Indeed, I cannot complain about anything today; it is everything one could ask for." She smiled at the sky and sighed happily.

Wellborne reined in his mount beside her side of the carriage. "It is perfect, is it not?"

"Indeed. Made to order. It is about time we had some nice weather. I have been sick to death of winter. I find it much more dreary in cities than in the country."

"I do, too. There is more to do in the country in the winter, somehow. What would you be doing at home in Londonderry this time of year?"

She was surprised that Mr. Wellborne would remember where they were from. "At home we always had so much to do that we hardly ever had time for pleasure excursions. In the city, one is expected to do nothing but amuse oneself, which gets very tiresome, especially when the weather is unpleasant. Right now at home I would be teaching French and Italian to some of the girls in the town, and seeing Papa's tenants, and going to meetings to plan for the charity bazaar which takes place later in the spring. What would you be doing at home if you were not here?" She squinted up to him in the bright sun.

Mr. Wellborne looked perplexed. "Nothing so worthy as yourself, I assure you. I am quite the wastrel, really." He smiled shamefacedly.

"You are from Yorkshire?"

"Scarborough."

"My father's family is from there. Perhaps you know the Yorkshire Montgomerys?"

"No. I don't. I haven't spent much time there lately." He shrugged. "But I have of course heard of your uncle Castlereagh."

Cassiopeia laughed. "Who hasn't, Mr. Wellborne? He is the Foreign Minister."

"Are you very close to him?" he asked.

"I suppose," Athena replied. "He and Aunt Castlereagh come out to Ireland every Christmas. Cass was supposed to have had a Season in London, but there were the Corn Riots, you know. Mama and Papa thought Bath would be better.''

"And then of course there is the rumor that Bonaparte has escaped,'' he said in a low voice.

"What do you mean?'' Cass demanded in alarm.

"I have only just heard, and I don't know if it is true, but it is said that Bonaparte left Elba at the end of February and has arrived in Cannes with eleven hundred men.'' He looked grim. "The news has only arrived this morning from London. Apparently the Corn Bill has been entirely forgotten.''

"Why would Napoleon go back to France? Surely they will only arrest him again.'' Cass darted a glance toward Monsieur Solage.

"That is the trouble. I hear that the common people still support him. He is trying to amass an army.''

"The real reason Uncle did not want us in London, I suspect,'' Athena murmured. "I wonder if he will be going back to Vienna to meet with the Peace Treaty committee. I'll wager they were not expecting this.''

"Are we going to war again?'' Cass's face puckered.

"Of course not. Boney will never raise an army. He will be clapped right back onto his island paradise. I hear he whiles away the time playing whist with his mother. Did you know she went into exile with him? The great emperor and his mama. I wonder if he brought his nursie too.'' Mr. Wellborne laughed and continued to soothe Cass's anxiety with an elaborate and fanciful description of Bonaparte's antics on Elba. Athena looked up at him admiringly. It was very kind of the Wellbornes to befriend them.

She wondered briefly if Charles and Cass might make a match of it. It wasn't likely to happen with Monsieur Solage around. Compared to the Frenchman, Wellborne seemed very ordinary. She glanced across to where Solage was riding on the opposite side of the carriage and found that he was looking at her intently. The left side of his mouth pulled into a mocking smile and his eyes flicked to Cass and Charles, who were laughing companionably. Hmph. So he was jealous, was he? Well, he deserved it. She suddenly felt very out of temper. She dragged her gaze away and forced herself to look out over the countryside.

The day could not have been finer. The breeze that had sprung up promised springtime and the sky was so clear that she fancied that she could see Bristol in the distance. It was hard to imagine that there could be anything wrong in the world.

When they reached the spot the Wellbornes had picked for the luncheon party, Athena jumped down from the carriage and drew a deep breath. No, she would not let Napoleon invade her thoughts today. Or anyone else. She helped her aunt out of the carriage and lead her over to where the men were beginning to pitch a canopy. They had decided against bringing the wheeled chair, but the elderly woman appeared to be able to manage on her own. It was remarkable what she had the health to accomplish when she felt so inclined. Celia Beetling, her mother, and several of their friends descended boisterously from the second carriage. The servants began to unload hampers of food from the cart that had followed the carriages.

"Well? What do you think of him? I don't need to ask what your sister thinks. One only needs to look at her." Auntie Montie gestured to where Cass was hanging off Monsieur Solage's arm and beaming up at him.

"What do I think of him?" Athena echoed. "He seems very pleasant." She mentally chastised Wellborne for allowing Solage to steal her sister away.

"Charming."

"Yes, very charming."

"Too charming," the woman snapped. "Mendacious."

Athena drew herself up. "I hardly think so. It perhaps only his Continental education that makes him seem . . . overly flattering."

"You don't educate insincere. I wouldn't be half surprised to find out he isn't quite what he says he is." A chair had been brought from the cart to the meadow chosen for the picnic and Auntie Montie leaned over and tested its stability.

"Don't tell me you have been listening to the idle gossip of the masses," Athena exclaimed with some asperity.

Auntie Montie gave a regal sniff. "There is no need to be impertinent, miss. I know a pretender when I see one." She lowered herself gingerly into the chair. "I'm likely to sink into the ground when I sit down. It's been so wet. What a foolish time for a picnic. Not halfway through March. We are more likely to get snow than sun," she grumbled. Apparently the conversation regarding Solage was closed.

Dominic allowed Miss Cassiopeia to tow him over to where Miss Montgomery was settling her aunt.

"Are you quite comfortable, Auntie?" she asked solicitously. "Perhaps you would like to rest here awhile with Athena. You could supervise the laying out of the food, Athena, since you are good at such things. Would you mind doing that while the rest of us take a look at the castle?"

"Well . . . no, I . . . well of course." He saw Athena look regretfully up at the castle. "I can look at it myself after lunch. I read a bit of its history yesterday in one of your books on Bath, Auntie."

"Pooh. Those books must be forty years old, girl. I don't know why I keep them. And I certainly don't know why you would want to be reading them."

She laughed. "The castle is far older than that, so I don't see why it should signify."

"Well when we get back, you can tell us what we have been looking at," Miss Cassiopeia said cheerfully. She turned to him, her eyes bright. "Athena will stay here with Auntie while the rest of us look at the castle." Her eyes were nearly the same color as her sister's, but there was something somehow more interesting about Miss Athena Montgomery's grave gray expression.

"But no, I cannot allow that," Dominic protested gently. "Miss Montgomery would surely like to see the castle herself." He bowed and caught a glimpse of her surprised face before he turned to her aunt. "And you, madam. Would you care to see it? You cannot have come all this way without wishing to look it over completely." He compressed his lips to hold back his laughter. It was obvious from the looks on both of their faces that they found his gallantries distasteful. *Dieu,* Miss Athena Montgomery would likely become a termagant, just like the old Miss Montgomery. When she talked of literature, those gray eyes sparkled with something that was almost like beauty, but now, when she was drawn up and prickling like a hedgehog, she was nothing but ordinary.

The older Miss Montgomery snorted. "You can be as elegant as you like Solage, you shan't turn me to toffee like these young creatures. I saw the castle once when I was my niece's age and there is no reason for me to have to see it again. I have no wish to totter about that dull, old pile. My legs are troubling me enough as it is."

"Indeed, madam. From what is it that you suffer?"

"Thrombosis mostly. My legs swell up like black puddings." She cackled at Miss Cassiopeia's faint gasp. "Ain't exactly what one should speak of I suppose, but in my day we weren't so missish."

Wellborne approached the little group. "Miss Montgomery, will you accompany us?'' he asked, smiling at her.

"No, I will stay here with my aunt. Do please continue on without me."

"I will stay here also," Dominic said. "We will form a second party for the visiting of the castle after lunch." He pulled over a chair and sat down decisively.

"Oh, but I was counting on you to come with us!" Cassiopeia was shrill in her disappointment. "Please do. Auntie and Athena will be just fine without us. In fact, they would probably prefer to supervise the setting out of the luncheon on their own."

"You must go on," he said firmly before Miss Montgomery could object. "I will supervise the building of a throne of cushions for you to seat yourself on when you return. You will be queen of the day, and we will tell stories for your amusement."

"Like in *The Decameron*," Athena chimed in.

"The what?"

"Do come on, Cass," Sophia called out from up the hill.

"Yes, yes, but I will only relinquish you, if I can really be queen of the day."

"You are queen of every day." He rose and bowed, and she smiled her dimpled smile and flounced up the hill.

"It is a good thing I haven't eaten or I should cast up my accounts," Auntie Montie snapped.

"Vomit," Athena supplied, in response to his bewildered expression.

"Queen of every day, indeed. You'll make that girl's head swell up like one of those hot air balloons. Doing it rather brown, Solage." Auntie Montie raised her lorgnette and examined him. "And don't you turn your roguish smile on me either. I know very well what you are up to.''

''Do you, madam? What am I up to, please?''

''No good,'' she replied tersely. ''Now get me a pillow for my feet.''

He obliged with a grin. ''My own grandmother has the thrombosis. She has had relief from it using the spa waters. Do you find the waters at Bath help you?'' he asked as he arranged the cushion under her feet. He saw from the corner of his eye that Athena's brows rose in amusement.

''No. But I find it much more comfortable to set up in my own household in Bath rather than live with some irritating relations. And they are all irritating, mind you.'' She leaned her head back in her chair and sighed with satisfaction.

''My grandmother also has a recipe for a poultice for the leg. It has given my godfather Lord Falk much relief.''

''I've known Falk these twenty years. And I never heard anyone talk of a French godson.'' She narrowed her eyes accusingly.

''Falk says you have not spoken to him these twenty years.''

''Hmph.'' She did not deny it. He wondered how much she knew. ''Thrombosis?'' she asked suddenly, returning to the question of the poultice.

''No, gout.''

Old Miss Montgomery had closed her eyes, but now they popped open again. ''What I need is something for thrombosis. I don't want any French quack cure for gout!''

''But it is good for all troubles of the legs. I will send the recipe over tomorrow. Whether you use it, or not, is up to you.'' He smiled and gave Athena a shameless wink over her aunt's head. She tried vainly to repress an answering smile.

''You can send it, but I won't use it. We'll try it out

on my butler Duncan though. He suffers from gout. If we can patch him up I won't have to pension him off, and I shall save a small fortune. I can see you smirking over there, missy. Oh yes, your aunt is an irascible old bird.'' She leaned her head back again and closed her eyes. ''Now you two busy yourselves setting out the luncheon and making that ridiculous throne of pillows for my silly niece. You know she took you literally, you silver-tongued rogue, and you will have to pay the price.'' She waved her hand imperiously, settled back, and pretended to go to sleep.

Poor old Miss Montgomery. He knew she was frustrated with the betrayal of her elderly body, and her sharp mind was too often bored by society's strictures. While she liked to style herself an eccentric crosspatch, he had seen right through her. Athena Montgomery, though, would not fare so well. She lacked her aunt's sense of humor. Oh yes, she might smile over a sally of his, but at heart she was entirely too serious for his taste.

He quickly piled several cushions into a semblance of a chair. ''Now, Miss Montgomery. I have finished my work, and I see that the servants are entirely capable of setting out the luncheon. You have no excuse to refuse a short stroll with me.'' He wished instantly that he hadn't offered. Castlereagh's niece, he reminded himself.

''You are very kind to offer, but I think that I should stay here.'' She pushed a strand of honey brown hair behind her ear in a businesslike manner and pretended to direct the servants in their work.

''Your aunt is asleep and cannot possibly need your assistance. We will not go far.'' He pointed silently at her aunt, who made a gesture of dismissal, though she valiantly kept her eyes closed.

Athena shrugged. ''Very well.'' She took his arm and they walked across the road to where a flower-filled meadow stretched out to a far line of trees. Butterflies tumbled about like live flowers in a frenetic dance. He felt strangely as though they were in another world, very far from that of aunts, sisters, and shipping companies.

"So tell me, Miss Montgomery, did you enjoy *Vathek* better than *The New Industrialism?*" he asked at last.

"Yes, though I have not had the chance to finish it."

"I am glad you enjoy it. If you like, I will loan you one of Descartes' works. You appear to me to be the kind of woman who would enjoy the philosophy. I would like to hear your opinion on the difference between the mind and the brain."

"You carried your books with you from France?" she asked in surprise.

He laughed softly. "Yes, I could not be without them. I left behind a fine stable of horses and a large house in the country, but I could not leave my books. It would injure their delicate sensibilities."

To his surprise, she laughed outright. It was the first time he had heard her do so. "I know just what you mean. Though it is foolish of me to think so. Does Falk not mind housing your books?"

He squinted up at the sun. Its heat made him feel languorously comfortable. "He has been very generous, my godfather. I am staying with him until my house here in Somerset is ready for my occupation. The place was left me by my mother. She was English. Did you know that?" Why was he confiding these things to her?

"No, I didn't."

He turned to look at her, but she seemed entirely absorbed in watching a butterfly that had landed on her sleeve. "I thought that everyone knew everything about me. Everywhere I go, people seem to know more about me than I do about myself."

"Bath is full of gossips. Please do not think that everyone is so nosy." The butterfly left her in favor of a daffodil, so she had no choice but to look up at him. Her gray eyes were sympathetic.

"Well then, you can be the first to publicize my new-found respectability. You would not know it from my English, for my mother died with I was quite young, and my father, he did not speak the language much better than myself. But indeed, I am half English and therefore at least half acceptable."

"It grieves me to hear you talk so." There was something so compelling about the calm depths of those eyes, that he forced himself to look away.

"Do not look so angry Miss Montgomery. I am well able to take care of myself in society." He grinned. "Though I would be delighted to have you as a champion, O Athena, warrior goddess."

"You are wicked to tease me. I cannot help it if I match my name all too well.

"Athena was also the goddess of wisdom," he reminded her.

She smiled wryly. "There are times when I wish I had a nice, plain name. 'Athena' gives me so very much to live up to."

"You very much looked like a warrior goddess when I first met you." She looked a bit like a goddess now, with a striking black and cerulean butterfly opening and closing its wings in her hair. He wondered what made him suddenly so fanciful. It wasn't like him.

She laughed and the creature fluttered around her head. "I was terrible. What an impression of me you must have had!"

"I had the impression that you were a terrifyingly intelligent woman." He thought of that first meeting. She hadn't turned out to be so very prim, dry, and humorless after all. She improved very much when she laughed.

"Terrifying? I am devastated!"

"I much admired the way you did battle with the shop-keeper." He shot her a look of pretend severity. "Even if I did not admire your taste in books."

"You are horrid! How many times do you wish for me to admit that you were right about the book?"

The butterfly continued dancing around her head. It looked like a tiny, shimmering stained-glass window. He wished he could catch it and show it to her. "Many, many times, as it is likely to be the last time I am right." Whoever had said that she was dull and plain had obviously never spent a moment in conversation with her.

The butterfly resettled on her shoulder.

She stopped still. "Look!" she whispered in awe.

He leaned closer to examine it. She smelled faintly of lavender.

"It must think I'm a flower. I look like a giant poppy."

He gingerly reached out a finger to the butterfly. The velvet of the coquelicot spencer she wore over her white lawn dress was soft against the back of his hand. She did not move away from him. The butterfly stepped onto his finger and he brought it around to show her.

"Ohhhh," she breathed out softly. She reached out a forefinger to the creature. Her fingers felt cool. "It looks very insecty up close, doesn't it?" She watched the butterfly with a fascinated half smile. She didn't look plain in the least.

"Yes."

"Remarkable."

"Yes." He leaned in closer.

The butterfly opened its brilliant wings and flitted off in a crazy dance. "Oh." She looked up a him in disappointment. "It's gone."

He stepped back and drew in a breath. She smiled

innocently up at him. "Well"—he cleared his throat—"we'd better go back."

"Perhaps so," she agreed reluctantly.

He did not offer her his arm on the way back, but she did not seem to notice. What had come over him? In another moment he would have kissed her. The prim little innocent probably had no idea how close he had been to taking her in his arms. She would most likely have boxed his ears in return, the termagant. He listened to her lecture on butterfly pupation with a frown. The irrational and unexpected attraction he felt must be instantly crushed. Castlereagh would not relish hearing rumors attaching his name with that of his niece. And the nature of his work on the Vienna Committee prevented him from even telling her that he knew her uncle. No, kissing was entirely out of the question.

"Do you know, Monsieur Solage," she interrupted her own discourse on entomology, "I like you very well when you are not bent on being flirtatious." She smiled her little half smile and then went to join her aunt.

Chapter Six

"You must see the castle. It is so very romantic!" Cass bounded over to where luncheon had been laid out, the daisies in her bonnet bobbing wildly. "You must run up there after our luncheon, Athena. Then you can come back and tell us all what we have seen. It is really a pity I did not read the guidebook, for I should love to know all of the history. I am sure it is full of scandal. Oh!" She ran up to where Monsieur Solage stood. "Is this my throne?"

"Indeed it is. You must seat yourself there like an Arabian princess. I shall procure a plate of food for you after your wanderings." Cass complied with an exclamation of delight, and her courtier set about dishing out food. Athena watched in annoyance. So much for him not playing the flirt.

"Doing it rather brown, wouldn't you say?" Mr. Wellborne asked quietly at her elbow.

"Very much so," Athena replied. Both he and Cass

were making a spectacle of themselves. She pushed the thought from her mind. "How did you enjoy the castle?"

"I found it sadly flat," he said with a doleful expression. "I had hoped that you would be one of the party. I had no intention that you be left behind to arrange the luncheon like a maiden aunt."

"I am the maiden aunt," she protested cheerfully, "or very nearly anyway. I did not mind in the least. I shall go and see the castle for myself after we have eaten."

"May I accompany you?"

Athena looked at him in surprise. "If you wish. Though I do not know why you would wish to see it twice in one day. Is it so very spectacular?"

He handed her a plate of food that he had filled for her and saw her settled comfortably on a cushion before he replied. "I must admit, Miss Montgomery, I should enjoy it more in your presence."

She felt a slight prickle of panic. What was wrong with everyone today? What happened to his interest in Cassiopeia? Was Wellborne showing an interest in *her*? Flirted with by two different men on the same day. It was unaccountably bizarre, and she was not sure if she enjoyed it or not. Besides, Solage had probably not been flirting with her at all. "You would like to know the history of the place, I suppose," she foundered, after a moment's awkward pause.

He looked at her with his blue eyes serious in his handsome face. "You are the only one of the party who read the history of the castle. I can only admire a woman of such intellect and forethought."

While it was a gratifying compliment, she was hard-pressed to suppress an exclamation of derision. Two days ago she would have been flattered indeed to be thought a woman of intellect and forethought. Now, she wanted to be something more. Oh yes, Athena, Warrior Goddess of Wisdom, she mocked herself mentally.

"As a woman of good education, you must enjoy talking with your uncle, Lord Castlereagh."

Her brows rose slightly. "Yes. When I get the chance. I have not had the opportunity to see him very much. He spends much of his time either in his constituency in Ireland or in London."

"You and Miss Cassiopeia are his only nieces, I believe?"

"We are. Why do you ask?"

He laughed, looking shamefacedly down at his plate. "Forgive me. I am overly inquisitive, I am afraid." His grin made him look very young. "I suppose I just want to know everything about you."

She dropped her head and picked at her food. His obvious attention should please her, but for some reason she only felt uncomfortable. If she ever had any intention of marrying, which she did not, Charles would have been perfect for her. He was a serious and sincere young man who seemed to hold her in esteem. Why did she feel like that was not enough?

"I have displeased you," Charles said abruptly. "I am very sorry, Miss Montgomery. Please forgive my impertinence."

Athena came back to herself and drew a deep breath of the springlike air. Cassiopeia and Sophia were laughing loudly over something Monsieur Solage had said. She found the noise suddenly grating. "Nothing of the sort," she said with a warm smile to Charles. "I am happy to talk of my family. Of course you would wish to know about my uncle, as he is a well-known man. I must warn you though that I do not agree with his politics. I am a firm Whig, and I support Princess Caroline's cause, even though he has done everything he can to thwart her."

He laughed. "Indeed. I applaud your sentiment. While I admire your uncle very much as a statesman, I, too, feel that the government should be more tolerant on the Catholic issue and address the working-class fears that have led to the Luddite riots. But, as worthy a debater as you may be, Miss Montgomery, I refuse to talk about politics when there is a beautiful castle to be seen on a perfect spring day." He stood and held out his hand to help her up. "Are you are finished with your luncheon? I would like to show you the castle, if you will tell me about the history."

Athena rose and pulled her spencer closer around her. "Of course. Shall we see who else would like to go?" She knew she could slip off with him to see the castle without causing too much comment. Really, at four-and-twenty she was quite on the shelf and beyond any touch of scandal. But she curiously felt no real desire to be alone with him.

"Monsieur Solage has not seen the castle. I will show it to him. Would you like that, sir?" Cass jumped up and attempted to pull the Frenchman to his feet. "Celia? Miss Wellborne? Would you like to come too?" Celia declined, preferring to sit in the sun with her mother and the rest of the guests. Sophia, however, took Monsieur Solage's other arm and accompanied them up the hill.

The party of three was not as eager to see the castle as herself though, and she and Mr. Wellborne soon found themselves well ahead of the group. Charles looked back over his shoulder and frowned.

"I confess, I cannot like Monsieur Solage."

"Why not?" Athena demanded. "He is exceedingly polite."

Charles looked slightly regretful. "I would not wish to speak ill of anyone, but I think that Solage is some-what . . . too charming."

"Nonsense." She chose not to remember that she had accused the Frenchman of the very same thing not but two days earlier. "Are you worried that Sophia may fall in love with him?"

He laughed. "No. My sister has too much sense for that. I . . ." He paused and awkwardly cleared his throat. "I am ashamed to speak of it, but I have heard that he is not the godson of Falk. That he has only used the story to gain entry into Bath society. Falk, as you know, is very reclusive because of his gout. He may not be aware that this insidious Frenchman is using his name."

"Insidious!" Athena objected indignantly. "I think the entire story nonsense. You refine too much upon him, Mr. Wellborne. Really, everyone in Bath has nothing on their minds but Monsieur Solage. I am sick to death of talking about him."

"I had such a marvelous time at the picnic last week, Miss Wellborne. We must thank you again for inviting us." Athena leaned back to keep her aunt's Bath chair from careening down the hill. She smiled at Sophia, who had joined the three Montgomery women on their daily sojourn to the Pump Room.

"Don't you dare let go, missy. I shall go flying all the way down the hill and into the Avon." Auntie Montie almost laughed at the mental picture. "You should have allowed the servant to push me. I never met a chit with more of an independent streak. What do you think I hire servants for, if not to push my Bath chair up and down to the Pump Room every day?"

"I can manage it, Auntie Montie. You can trust me."

Cass shot her sister a wicked glance, suggesting that she herself would not be so trustworthy, but helped her sister control the chair's descent. "We did have a fine day, Sophia. What a grand idea. I think we should make a point of picnicking every week. Think of all the nice places we could visit, now that the weather is getting finer!''

"We know your reasons for having a good time on the excursion," Auntie Montie cackled. "Slow down. With the two of you heaving back there, you're like enough to dump me into the street. Stop your giggling, missy"—she jerked her head over her shoulder to glower at Cass—"or I'll write to your mother and tell her that you have been behaving like a complete hoyden. Not as though she would care; that woman was always far more interested in her treatises than child-rearing.''

"True," Cassiopeia agreed cheerfully. "But I shall find a husband this season and then everyone will be satisfied.''

"I can't imagine who would want to marry a silly creature like you. But apparently I am the only one. The house is full to bursting with your suitors. Rattles every one of them. I notice Monsieur Solage has been absent though.''

Athena found that her aunt's sharp eyes were upon her rather than Cass. She blinked back in astonishment.

"He has gone out of town," Cass replied, pertly. "And more is the pity, for he might find me engaged upon his return.''

"Do you really think that he could be a French spy?" Sophia asked in an awed voice.

Athena lifted her shoulders. "No."

"There is something havey-cavey about him," Auntie Montie argued. "I have no doubt that he is not who he says he is.''

"Nonsense!" Athena surprised herself with the vehemence of her own exclamation. "The French have no need for spies. Napoleon shall be stopped in a day or two. A troop is going to Grenoble at this moment to arrest him. We may find Solage's Continental manners somewhat overly complimentary and, of course, he is a good deal too charming to be sincere, but there is no need to submit to rampant ignorance and fear.''

It was as if no one had heard her. Auntie Montie merely looked at her intently as her lips twisted into a peculiar smile.

"I think it would be highly romantic if he were to be a spy,'' Cass announced as she stepped back to allow two attendants to lift the Bath chair over the doorsill of the Pump Room. "Or a smuggler at the very least. Then perhaps he would be shot and I could nurse him back to health. I think that I should enjoy that very much.''

"How is your brother, Sophia?'' Athena interrupted.

"Very well indeed. He sent his regards. You will see him tonight if you are going to the assembly.''

Athena could see Cass making a face of arch interest over Sophia's shoulder. It was very similar to the expression Auntie Montie had made a moment before. "I am not certain that we will be going,'' she murmured, feeling very self-conscious.

"Miss Wellborne, I have been meaning to ask you. Are you related to the Gerald Wellbornes?'' Auntie Montie said suddenly.

"No, ma'am. I believe they spell their name differently,'' Sophia replied.

The old woman smiled benignly. "Then you must be one of the Bertram Wellbornes. I know them well. Lady Wellborne went to school with me.''

Sophia's brows rose. "No, ma'am. I don't believe we are related to them.''

"They are from Scarborough, I believe. Are you not from Scarborough, Miss Wellborne?''

Athena felt acutely embarrassed as she saw Sophia's

color rise. What was her aunt thinking, quizzing her friend like this!

"We are from a small town not far from Scarborough. I doubt that you would know it."

"On the contrary, I know Scarborough well. The girls' father and I have connections in that part of the country. I am certain I would know your people."

"I am from Cayton. But my family moved around quite a lot. Perhaps you would not remember my family." Looking very upset, Sophia scanned the room for someone to rescue her.

"And what is your father's name?" Auntie Montie persisted mercilessly.

"It is—it is—Michael," she stammered.

"Perhaps you would like to take a turn around the room, Auntie." Athena forcibly wheeled her aunt away. "What ever made you act such a terrible quiz!" she scolded. "Miss Wellborne has been nothing but kind to Cass and me."

"Miss Wellborne indeed. She isn't from Scarborough. She is most likely not a Wellborne. In fact, she is likely not well born at all!" The old woman laughed her strange, silent laughter at this pun. "Heh heh! Not well born indeed! I fancy she is some creature of unknown origins who made up the name to foist herself upon the world."

"Auntie! Please do not continue this conversation with me. I consider Sophia Wellborne my good friend, regardless of her family connections."

"I'm not such a high stickler. I just don't like this bald-faced lying. If she is some nobleman's bastard, what do I care?"

Athena gasped. "I cannot believe I am hearing such things! I don't know how you can doubt her—her origins when she seems so very well bred and her brother is so very—"

"Ah yes, her brother. There is something strange about him as well. But of course the both of them have pulled the wool over your eyes."

"I will speak no more on this subject!" Athena hissed.

"Then what of Solage?"

"What of him?" Her head was beginning to ache. Trust Auntie Montie to bring up these subjects in public places.

"Where is *he* from? Who are *his* people? I never heard Falk had a godson. Why is he off to London once a week? There is something havey-cavey going on there too."

Athena could not help but laugh. "Oh, Auntie, we shall have such fun when I am your companion. Just think of all the lies we can make up about people. You will have the news from every gossip in town, and then you can send me out to investigate all the nefarious pretenders who have invaded Bath!"

He first caught sight of Miss Montgomery as she made her way down the hill on Gay Street. Her poor maid trailed behind her, panting. Something about the thin, sharp air of early spring suited Athena. Her cheeks were pink and she was swinging the books she held while she hummed happily to herself.

He hoped that she would not see him, but she did. She looked as though she was not sure if she was glad to see him or not. "How do you do, Miss Montgomery?" he asked with forced joviality. After he had spent the rest of the picnic flirting outrageously with every other woman but her, he wasn't likely to get a warm reception. It was of little moment. He had more important things on his mind than the opinion of a charmingly starchy bluestocking.

"Very well. How are you?"

"Very well indeed." They smiled awkwardly in the silence.

"How did you find London?"

How did she know that was where he had gone? "It was a very pleasant trip." He hoped she did not ask for more information.

"I hear that the town was in an uproar over Napoleon when the news came out that the army sent to arrest him at Grenoble has now joined him."

He choked back a reply. *Dieu,* but it would be interesting to find out what she thought about the recent developments. He shrugged. "I cannot talk about politics when I am in the company of a beautiful woman." She already thought him a flirtatious rattle; this should infuriate her.

"Indeed." Her repressive reply showed that he was right.

"Where are you going?"

"I must stop at the apothecary's shop, and then I am going to the lending library."

"You are always with the books." He mocked her with a smile. "I heard it said that you were a bluestocking, and I did not know what the word meant. Bluestocking," he said the word carefully. "But I have found out that it is only from the poem 'Bas-Bleu' and has nothing to do with your legs at all." He made a face of profound disappointment.

She did not reply.

"Do you wear blue stockings, Miss Montgomery?" He stopped himself from asking teasingly for a viewing of her stocking, blue or not. He did not relish a slap in the face.

"I will ignore that question, Monsieur Solage," she replied primly.

"Then I will ask you another. Where is your sister?"

She did not appear to like this question any better. "She is at home. She will be sorry that she was not here to meet you. Shall I convey a message to her?"

"No, It is you I wished to see."

"Me?" Her voice came out breathlessly.

He thought of a reason quickly. "I wished to offer to you a book of mine. Descartes. I thought that it might interest you."

"Yes, of course. I would like that very much," she replied. She was once again her cool, removed self.

"I would value your comments. It is a pleasure indeed to converse with someone as well-read as yourself."

"You flatter me, sir."

"Indeed I do not. You will permit me to bring the book to the Royal Crescent then?" *Diantre*, why couldn't he stay away from her?

"Of course. We are always delighted to see you. Though I must warn you, Auntie does not like visitors. Here is Mr. Whitley's." She stopped abruptly at the door of the apothecary's shop.

"Then I will wish you good day and hope for the happiness of seeing you very soon."

"I hope so, too, Monsieur Solage. Thank you very much for accompanying me." Her smile when she gave him her hand to shake turned into an expression of annoyance when he carried it to his lips. He shouldn't have worried. Castlereagh's niece could be depended upon to squash any of his pretensions if he were ever again to be so foolish as to forget himself.

Chapter Seven

Athena entered the shop and stood for a moment with her hands pressed to her cheeks, willing them to cool. What an odious man! It was obvious that, realizing her countrified naiveté, he delighted in putting her out of countenance with an excess of Continental charm. How utterly annoying. Cass should be forewarned that not a sincere word would come out of that man's mouth. Betty caught her eye and wiggled her ginger eyebrows expressively. Athena tried to frown, but the attempt was a considerable failure.

Lady Battford and her two daughters recognized Athena as she entered the shop and called out their greetings.

"Was that Monsieur Solage I saw with you?" Miss Battford asked, wide-eyed.

"It was."

The two young ladies each clasped one of her arms and bent their heads toward hers. "How very dashing he is, to be sure!'' Miss Sarah said in an excited undertone. ''Do you think he is a spy?''

''Of course not. He is half English.''

''Is he indeed?'' Her brows rose in surprise. ''But he is also half French.'' They lowered again meaningfully.

''And your uncle is Castlereagh! He must have been hoping to find out state secrets!'' Miss Battford squeezed Athena's arm painfully.

''Yes, who better to court than the niece of the Foreign Minister!'' her sister continued. ''I'll wager he is reporting back to Napoleon himself.''

''He is not courting me.'' She felt her neck go hot with a blush.

Miss Battford looked shocked. ''I should think not. That would be very peculiar indeed. Sarah meant Miss Cassiopeia of course. Does she favor him?''

Athena choked out some sort of negative reply.

''What were you talking about just now? Did you tell him anything important?'' Miss Sarah tittered.

''Just think! Anything you tell him might be told to that Corsican monster. Our very security could depend on you! He could descend any day on our heads!''

Athena's arm was beginning to ache from Miss Battford's vice grip. ''Indeed, Bath is a hotbed of national secrets,'' she said dryly.

Miss Sarah squealed. ''I have the most marvelous idea! You could give him false information! You could tell him that Wellington has simply heaps of troops in the west when they are actually in the east or some such thing!''

''I have no idea where the troops actually are in France.'' She attempted to remove herself from the sisters' clutches.

''No? Does your uncle not tell you? I thought that, as

you are so very . . . well, so very bookish, your uncle might discuss such things with you.''

"Indeed he does not. It would be very inappropriate.''

"No? Well I should think that you would be able to make something up. You being so frighteningly clever and all.'' Miss Sarah's lower lip began to protrude in a pout. "I hope he will speak to me at the next assembly. My brother has met him and has promised to introduce both Anne and myself. I am quite wild to meet an actual spy.''

"Well, I am afraid that you are highly unlikely to do so in Bath,'' Athena replied tartly.

"Girls! Do stop your chattering. I declare you give me the headache with your incessant natterings. We were expected at Lady Reading-Thrandle's house nearly half an hour ago. Come along this instant.'' Lady Battford relentlessly towed away her protesting daughters.

Athena watched them go and then let the smile drop from her face. How dare they propagate such slander! The very idea that a French spy would find it worth his while to infiltrate the stuffy echelons of Bath society was laughable indeed. After all, London society was positively littered with French émigrés come to England during the Revolution. She completed her errand with Mr. Whitley and continued on to the lending library.

Monsieur Solage had said that he was living with his godfather, Lord Falk. She knew the name of the elderly, vociferous member of the House of Lords from the papers. Her uncle was actually quite a crony of his. Her steps slowed. Perhaps . . . perhaps she could write Uncle Castlereagh and ask if he knew any particulars of Monsieur Solage. She stopped on the sidewalk and gave herself a mental shake. That was ridiculous. She scowled at her reflection in the window of a milliner's shop. If anyone was behaving like a sneaky little spy, it was she!

Monsieur Solage was entirely trustworthy and there was no cause to doubt it. It was only gossipmongers like the Battford sisters who would ever think of something so ludicrous based solely on where he was from. Her frown deepened. She would put the entire upsetting experience from her mind.

"Betty," she said firmly, "I am going to buy a new bonnet."

"Athena!" Cass looked up from her book in surprise. "What is that you are wearing on your head?"

Athena reached up gingerly to touch the bonnet trimmed with midnight blue ribbons. "Oh dear, is it that bad? And I had grown so very fond of it."

Her sister leapt to her feet and came up to examine it. "It is very dashing indeed," she breathed in admiration. "Did you pick it out? You have marvelous taste when you put your mind to it. I am so glad you took my advice to get a new one. The old thing was quite out of fashion, you know."

"I am glad you approve." She took off the bonnet with some reluctance and handed it carefully to Betty. "What have you been up to?"

Cass gave a peculiar start. "Nothing," she said quickly. "It has been very dull indeed." She shot her sister an arch smile. "But *you* have had a visitor." She laughed at Athena's look of surprise. "Indeed, Lord Falk's footman brought by a book for you. Monsieur Solage is staying with Falk, you know." She flung herself onto the settee and put her hand to her forehead dramatically. "You have stolen my beau!"

"Hardly," Athena scoffed. She had somehow thought that Monsieur Solage meant to bring the book by himself. Of course, it was much more convenient for him to have his man deliver it. How silly of her to have thought otherwise.

"I have decided that I will marry him."

Athena's head snapped up. "What?"

"I have decided to marry Monsieur Solage," she repeated happily. "I should be quite the envy of Bath, don't you think? Do you suppose he will tell me the great secrets of the French Empire when we are married?"

Athena felt as though she was choking. "Do you love him?" she managed at last.

"Passionately!" Cass waved her hand airily. "I have yet to write Mama and Papa, of course, as he has not exactly proposed, but I suspect they shall be relieved to find I am off their hands so quickly."

"Proposed!" Athena echoed stupidly.

Cass laughed. "You look a complete goose with your mouth hanging open like that. No, Solage has not proposed, but I suppose he will very soon." She shrugged and picked up a book of fashion plates.

Athena stared at her. She felt as though she had inadvertently skipped a few pages in a book during an important turning point in the plot. Was it possible that Monsieur Solage was in love with Cass? He had mentioned her this morning, but ... She felt a knot of worry form in her stomach. Either Cass had mistaken Solage's attention and was about to make a cake of herself by flinging herself at him, or he was actually in love with her. She ruthlessly forced herself to smile. "I am not so anxious to be rid of you, Cass. Promise me that you will make certain that your heart is engaged before you accept any offer."

Reminding herself that her sister understood men far better than she did herself, she picked up the book that Solage's man had brought by and pulled herself tiredly up the stairs to her room. She opened the book and began unbuttoning her gray pelisse with one hand. The leather binding of the book hinged smoothly, but the scent from the pages proclaimed this a vintage printing. She brought the book to her nose and inhaled deeply.

She dropped the pelisse onto the settee and curled up in the old wingback by the fire. Solage had written his name on the front page of the book. Dominic Solage. The handwriting was bold and slanted heavily to the right. Dominic. She felt strange knowing his first name. It struck her that if Cassiopeia was right, he would be her brother-in-law. They would spend holidays together, and she would be aunt to his children. She would end up the poor spinster sister, dependent on the charity of Monsieur and Madame Solage. The knot in her stomach returned.

Forcing herself to put these thoughts from her mind, she resolutely turned the page. A half sheet of paper slipped from the book and fell to the floor. It skittered across the carpet and landed underneath the chaise. Torn for a moment whether to bother about it or not, Athena reluctantly got up and retrieved it. It was written in the same strong hand as the name in the front of the book. But this was not Solage's name—it was a list of names. She sat down bonelessly on the floor. Four of the seven names belonged to powerful men in Parliament. One of those was her uncle Castlereagh. The other three were men entirely unconnected to the government.

Unconnected unless one knew of the Vienna Committee.

She sagged against the leg of the chaise. Was it possible that Solage knew of the committee her uncle had formed upon his return from Vienna? He had collected a group of men who were otherwise unconnected, to gather information on England's resources. He knew Wellington could not count on the war being fought as it had been in Spain. The French general would have learned from his mistakes. The guerrilla-style warfare of the Spanish dissidents would be entirely different from the new front forming in the east of Europe.

How could Solage know of the Committee? She herself knew of its existence only because Castlereagh had called upon her parents to examine Napoleon's Ionian Island occupation of 1809. He had hoped their knowledge of Greek language and culture would help him assess that country's ability to withstand a second assault from France. But Solage?

"Impossible!" she said aloud, but instead of sounding indignant, she heard her voice shake weakly. Could he really be . . . She wouldn't even let her mind form the words. A scratch on the door startled her out of her stunned trance.

Betty stuck her head in the door and grinned. "Your aunt is wanting you, miss. She's in quite a state."

Athena got to her feet, happy to have something else to focus her thoughts on. It was simply a coincidence and she would put it from her mind. Perhaps the Vienna Committee was not as much of a secret as she had thought.

"Did you get my tonic?" Auntie Montie demanded stridently. "I'm weak as a cat today."

Athena gave a forced laugh. "Indeed you are. So infirmed that you threatened to box Dr. Lightner's ears this morning if he did not change your medicine."

Auntie Montie frowned away the smile that was invading her thin lips. "Enough impertinence from you, miss. Did you—"

"Yes, I have the tonic and yes, I did remember to take Betty with me." Athena picked up the cashmere shawl her aunt had flung over the back of the chaise and arranged it around the woman.

Perhaps Solage had heard of the Committee from his godfather. That was surely the answer. Lord Falk was highly influential in Parliament. The handwriting on the list might even belong to him.

"Miss Athena, Miss Wellborne is here to see you," Betty announced from the doorway.

"Could you ask Miss Cassiopeia to go to her? I am not yet finished with my aunt." She felt a faint surge of guilt. She had been taken on as a companion to Auntie Montie, but most of her time had been spent chaperoning Cass. Auntie was getting impatient with the constant callers.

Perhaps the Vienna Committee had been dissolved and the ex-members were freed from their bonds of secrecy.

"Miss Cassiopeia is out driving with Lord Aston." Betty stood on one foot, waiting for an answer.

Perhaps Solage actually was a spy. She pictured his face with his dark brown eyes that always seemed to be laughing at her. Did spies have a sense of humor?

"For the love of Murphy!" Auntie Montie exploded. "The house is full to bursting every minute with infernal visitors. I never should have taken you two girls in. I told Cass this morning that if she was not married by spring, I shall send you both back to Londonderry. I will not have my peace disrupted every moment with these hordes of admirers." The woman fretfully twisted a corner of the shawl. "I wanted a companion, not a traveling stage show!"

"Please sent my regrets to Miss Wellborne, and tell her that I will be happy to call upon her some other time." She had never been to the house where Charles and Sophia lived with their grandmother.

Perhaps Solage did not actually live with Lord Falk after all. His lordship's health was not very good and he was rarely seen in public. As Charles had said, he might not have heard that there was an impostor using his name to gain entree.

"Oh go down to her," Auntie Montie snapped. "I don't want you here if you are going to be distracted. You've had a completely absorbed look on your face from the moment you walked into the room. I won't spend my time talking to a post, thank you." She made an impatient gesture of dismissal and closed her eyes.

Athena watched her for a moment, but as the old woman did not renege on her command, she went downstairs to greet Sophia.

"How are you, Athena? It has been an age since I have seen you. How is your sister and aunt?"

"They are both well. And your family?"

"They are well. Charles asked me to convey his particular inquiries after you." Sophia smiled archly, but Athena pretended not to notice. "What is wrong?" she demanded suddenly.

"Why, nothing,"

"What a bounder! You are white as talc! Has something happened?"

"No indeed. I am quite well. It is just—"

"What? You know I am only teasing about Charles. I never meant to upset you." Sophia took her arm and led her to a seat.

"No, it is not that." She collapsed gratefully on the upholstered bench against the wall. It would not be wise to tell anyone of her finding when she did not know its origin, but she desperately needed someone else's advice. "I have found something that belongs to Monsieur Solage," she said slowly. "And I am not at all sure what it means."

Chapter Eight

"A spy!" Sophia breathed rapturously.

Athena leaned back against the wall, feeling suddenly tired. "No, now I didn't say that. I only said that I did not know how he could have gotten the list of names."

"How else could he? No one else knew."

"Well, if I knew, it could not be so very secret. I am certain there are many reasons he might have such a list." Her fingers slid to the pocket in her skirts where she had hidden the slip of paper. She longed to burn the wretched thing and forget that she had ever seen it.

"Tell me who is on it!" Sophia clasped her hands.

"No. I am sorry, but I cannot. Only believe me when I tell you that it was a list of people who are otherwise unconnected with each other and who have been gathered together by my uncle for a government committee. I really know little more than that, Sophia, and I don't feel as though I should speak of it. I should not have told you, except that I am confused about what to do." She stood up and paced the length of the room. "Should I tell Uncle Robert about it? Should I say nothing?" She had thought she would feel better if she shared her secret with Sophia, but she did not. Now she felt as though she had somehow betrayed Uncle Robert *and* Monsieur Solage.

"If only there was some way we could check into Solage's background." Sophia clasped her hands and looked up at Athena with an excited sparkle in her blue eyes.

"I hardly think that that would be appropriate. Besides, we do not know anyone who is connected with him"— she thought for a moment—"except for Lord Falk."

"Exactly!"

"But I have never been introduced to him, and I would wager you have never been either. We cannot just traipse up to him and begin asking impertinent questions about his godson."

"If indeed Solage is his godson. Falk's gout is so bad that he rarely goes out at all. It would be very easy indeed for someone to pose as his godson. Solage hardly runs in the same circle of ancient cronies who know Falk!" Sophia suddenly jumped up and clapped her hands. "What a splendid idea! I will get my bonnet!"

"What are you talking about?"

"We are going to ask Lord Falk about Monsieur Solage!"

Athena regarded her with disbelief. "Are you entirely mad? I admire the rapid and fanciful nature of your imagination, but you must see that this is entirely inappropriate. I was thinking that at most, I would write a discrete letter to my uncle, asking him exactly how secret the committee was, but not mentioning that I had come across the list. How foolish we are being! No spy would be so utterly careless as to leave a list of important information in the pages of a book he intended to loan out to the niece of the Foreign Minister! I'll wager it is a coarse jest designed to make us fly into a tizzy.''

''I'm in quite a tizzy,'' Sophia admitted cheerfully. ''And nothing you can say will absolve Solage of spying until I hear it from his godfather's mouth that he is above-board.''

''Of course!'' Athena's shawl dropped to the floor as she stood in stunned enlightenment. ''The book belongs to Falk! He is on the Committee himself, and that is why, of course, he has a list with everyone on the Committee but himself!'' She sat down on the bench again in an attitude of complete serenity.

''Are you certain that Lord Falk is on the Committee?'' Sophia looked intensely disappointed.

''Well''—she leaned over and retrieved her shawl from the floor—''I don't know for certain. I only heard the list of names mentioned once. It might have been incomplete.'' She draped it carefully from her elbows, waiting anxiously for the crow of triumph that was sure to come.

''Ah-hah!''

Athena cringed. ''I refuse to be a part of your scheming, Sophia.''

A quarter of an hour later she was trudging up the steps of the imposing house on Rivers Street. Sophia had already rapped an aggressive tattoo on the door and stood expectantly before it with her feet wide apart in an almost military stance. After an interminable amount of fumbling with a series of locks, an ancient butler swung the door open. He squinted at the two young women for a long moment and his long eyebrows shifted upward.

''I am Miss Wellborne, and this is Miss Montgomery. Is Lord Falk at home?'' Sophia asked sweetly.

''You miss your home?'' he shouted. ''Who are you? Why have you come to tell us that you miss your home? This is Lord Falk's home!''

"Is Lord Falk at home?" Athena repeated loudly.

"Yes, this is Lord Falk's home! That's what I told you before! What's wrong with you girls? Bedlamites!"

"Lord Falk . . ." she tried again.

"He's gone to London! Won't be back until Sunday!"

Athena and Sophia exchanged glances and shrugged slightly. "Well at least we have the right house," Sophia murmured with an impish smile.

"Lighthouse? Get out of here or I'm going to call the watch." The butler glowered at them and then slammed the door. They heard the scraping litany of door locking begin.

Sophia collapsed into a fit of giggles and Athena sagged against the area railing in relief. "I suppose that is the end of our misadventures." She laughed weakly.

"I should think not!" Sophia protested. "I am dead set on finding out if Solage is indeed a spy. Now that we know that Falk is out of the house . . ." Her voice trailed off suggestively.

Athena gave a low moan, attached herself firmly to Miss Wellborne's elbow, and pulled her friend forcibly back up the street.

Dominic Solage stepped down from the post chaise and absently dusted off his breeches. This traveling back and forth to London every week was hell. Next time he would hire a hack. Perhaps he would even look into buying a mount. He smiled a tight half smile at the thought. It was about time he resigned himself to the commitment of keeping a few possessions. For the past six years he had owned nothing but a few changes of clothes. And the books. His taut smile relaxed into one of pleasure. It was good to have them. Most of them had been in the attic of a rundown boarding house since . . . well since a long time ago.

He ran his fingers through his hair, replaced his hat, and walked briskly up High Street. Athena would enjoy Descartes. Not Athena, Miss Montgomery, he chided himself. She would never be the pretty English rosebud her sister was, but there was a depth to her, a depth to those mercury-colored eyes. . . . He laughed aloud at himself. There was plenty to think of, without waxing poetic over the prim Miss Athena Montgomery's solemn gray eyes.

Well in any case, she made Bath bearable. He actually found himself looking forward to getting back. That and looking for the deWit brothers. Falk was growing impatient with his lack of progress.

"Monsieur Solage! Thank heaven I have found you!" He staggered under the sudden weight attached to his right arm.

"Miss Cassiopeia Montgomery!" he exclaimed, wondering briefly how he had managed to conjure her up. "How are you? Where is your sister?" He looked about and found her quite on her own.

"Monsieur Solage! You must help me!" She gave a shudder and threw herself into his arms.

After briefly glancing around for help, he gingerly patted her on the back. "My dear mademoiselle, what is the matter? Are you hurt?"

She sobbed for a moment into his neck cloth before she was able to reply. "I . . . I am lost!" She detached herself enough to be able to look up at him, her eyes swimming in tears. "I went out for a walk with my maid, and she has abandoned me. She—she met her sweetheart, Mr. Cox, the apothecary's assistant, and he was walking with us and—and somehow they managed to lose themselves!" She pressed her trembling body against him again. She looked up in dismay when he began to laugh.

"You have lost yourself in Bath?"

"Indeed, sir! I am entirely alone and so frightened!"

"In Bath?" he asked incredulously. "It is my impression that no one is ever alone or lost in Bath. On the contrary, everyone seems to know exactly what everyone else is doing all the time. The capitol of busybodies, Bath." He stepped away from her and offered her his handkerchief. "Nothing terrible has befallen you?"

"I—I—But you must help me, Monsieur Solage! I should deem it a great service if you could return me to my aunt's house. I should owe you"—she drew a shaking breath and prettily dabbed her eyes with the handkerchief—"a great deal." She must have known the tears still clung to her upper lashes.

"Of course I will aid you. How could I resist such an entreaty?" He took her hand and led her to where a pair of chairmen were leaning against their sedan chair and leisurely smoking their pipes. "Please convey this young lady to the Royal Crescent." He tossed a coin to the front man.

"You would put me in a chair?" Cassiopeia demanded sharply.

Solage turned to her and bowed with a look of surprise. "Forgive me, mademoiselle. I thought that you wished to be conveyed home with the greatest speed. The chairmen will take you home in much less time than it would take for me to escort you, and surely you are tired from so much walking about being lost. You will take comfort, of course, that this way will also ensure that you are not seen walking unescorted with a virtual stranger. If you prefer it, however, I would be happy to escort you on foot."

"I'll take the chair," she replied tartly, seating herself in it with a flounce.

"I shall follow to make certain that you are conveyed

home safely." He bowed over her hand, glad that it con-
cealed the amused smile that he was finding hard to suppress. The foolish creature had made a bold play for him
indeed. Could she actually have conceived a schoolgirl's
tendre for him? Or was she attracted by the dangerous
rumors attached to his name? The smile was replaced by
the thin line of his compressed lips. Any more gossip and
he would be off the Committee.

"Don't trouble yourself." She pulled the door closed
and sat looking stonily ahead as the chairmen lifted her
up.

"But indeed I will. I must make sure that this precious
cargo is not lost again. Though, as you manage to look
even more beautiful when you are distressed, perhaps it
would be worth it." There. That should please her. He
tipped his hat to her and obediently followed the sedan
chair up the hill. Perhaps Athena would be home when
he returned her sister to her. Perhaps she was very worried
about her sister and would fly at him in gratitude when
he returned the girl to her home. She was so slight, he
would be able to enfold her in his arms completely. No.
He would not think about that. There were a good many
other things to worry about than seducing the fascinating
English bluestocking. He had a service to provide for his
country. His smile was grim. It was as unlikely to reward
him with fulsome thanks as the remote and collected Miss
Montgomery.

"Cassiopeia! Where have you been? Your maid came
home fully an hour ago and would not say a word!"
Athena had rushed downstairs when she saw her sister
get out of the chair and opened the door of the house.
Cass did not reply, but looked back over her shoulder.
Athena followed her glance and saw Monsieur Solage

cresting the hill. She suddenly felt unaccountably unwell. Before she could formulate the question she was not sure she wanted to know the answer to, Solage smiled, swept off his hat, and gave a low bow. Then, he turned abruptly on his heel and strode off down the hill. "What is going on?" she demanded.

"Oh, Athena! I have made such a hash of things!" Cass wailed.

"Well don't shout it out here on the doorstep." She ushered her inside and untied the ribbons of her bonnet for her. "Come upstairs to my room and tell me." She handed Cass's bonnet to the butler, who had only now emerged from belowstairs, and pulled her sister up the stairs.

Once in her room, Cass slumped into a chair and looked miserable. "You are going to be very cross with me," she warned.

Athena sat down across from her sister with a composure she did not feel. "Tell me what has happened."

"I did not go out to meet a school friend, as I told you I was going to do," she began, stubbing the toe of her slipper into the peony pattern of the rug. "I went out to meet Monsieur Solage."

Athena was reminded of the time as a child she had fallen out of a tree and landed flat on her back. She couldn't draw a breath properly. She managed to nod at Cass to continue.

"I had my maid go round to his house and she found that he was in London, but would be back this afternoon. We waited at the posting house until we saw him arrive." Cass looked up to assess how the story was being received and then dropped her eyes back to the carpet. "When he did arrive, I followed him and then pretended that I had gotten lost."

"In Bath?" Athena exclaimed.

Cass laughed ruefully. "It is a ridiculous idea, I know. But at the time, it seemed to make sense. I thought that if he believed that Betty had run off with her beau, and I was all alone . . ."

"He would be obliged to rescue you," she finished. She sat up straighter and squared her shoulders. "I am sure he was charmed to be able to render you a service. However, Cass, I am sure you know how extremely devious that was. Certainly Monsieur Solage has paid you a good deal of attention without you needing to resort to subterfuge."

"Don't scold. I know it was wicked. I just"—Cass kicked the peony again—"I just needed to see him alone."

"Why?" She gasped. "What has happened?" Several unpleasant possibilities invaded her head.

Cass flopped back into her chair with a dramatic sigh. "Nothing," she announced flatly. "I was hoping that if he saw me alone he might make a declaration."

"Of what?"

Cass rolled her eyes. "You haven't a heart in your body, Athena. All you care for are your dry old books. I was hoping that he would make a declaration *of love!* I was hoping that he would *propose.*" She allowed her head to loll over so that she could see her sister's reaction.

"Propose what?"

"What?" she shrieked in dismay.

Athena laughed as she got up to stoke the fire. "I am teasing you, Cassiopeia. I know very well what you meant." Solage must not have proposed or Cass would not be so disgruntled. But if Cass had set her sights on him, it was only a matter of time before he fell victim to her charms. No heart indeed! She gave the fire a few more vicious stabs, glad that her sister could not see her face.

"I should hope so! Well, in case you were wondering if you should wish me happiness, you should not. The horrid creature very nearly mocked me for being lost in Bath, though I suppose that was a very stupid excuse, and then he *sent me home in a chair!*"

Athena turned to see her sister's comic expression of dismay. Only the knowledge that this was but a temporary setback kept her from laughing aloud. "I am sorry you were thwarted," she said gravely.

Cass giggled. "I *was* thwarted." She repeated the word in a tone of self-mockery. "And I feel very foolish. Please don't tell Auntie Montie."

"Of course not. But why did you do it?" She cleared her throat, since it felt as though it was closing. "Have you developed a *tendre* for him?"

Her sister gave another heavy sigh. "I suppose," she said peevishly. "I don't really know. I only know that I will not be sent back to Londonderry."

"What are you talking about?"

"Auntie Montie says that she will pack us both back home if I am not married inside of two months. I like Monsieur Solage very well, and he seemed to like me, at least I thought he liked me until today. Today he treated me like a child. I suppose I was acting like a child, but still; it was most provoking! I thought perhaps, since he has always paid me the most extravagant compliments, that he was perhaps a little in love with me, and therefore would not mind too much marrying me." She looked up at Athena, her pretty round face nearly upside down over the arm of the chair.

Athena knelt down by her sister's chair and took her hand. "Cassie, don't listen to a word Auntie Montie says. You do not have to marry anyone you do not wish to."

Cass sat up and shook her honey-colored curls into

place. ''But I wish to marry Monsieur Solage,'' she said simply.

Betty entered the room. She saw Athena and looked a little sheepish.

''Mr. Wellborne is here to see you, Miss Montgomery,'' she managed to bleat out before she fled the room.

''Drat that man! I don't wish to deal with him now.''

''Athena! I thought he was your beau! I thought you liked him!''

''I—I don't know,'' she sputtered.

''Good heavens!'' Cass blinked innocently. ''I should have thought you would be happy to have someone courting you. Especially since he is the first beau you have ever had.''

Athena shot her a look of fury and left her sister protesting violently that she had not meant it to sound quite like that.

Chapter Nine

"Hello, Mr. Wellborne. How kind of you to come to see us. I hope that you are well?" She managed the civilities in a brittle tone.

"I am very well indeed. But I must correct you. I came to see you. No one else." He smiled fondly down at her.

She dropped her gaze to his cravat. "How very kind of you," she repeated awkwardly. "Shall I ring for tea?"

As she reached out for the bellpull, he took her hand and pressed it. "Don't. Let us take a turn in the garden instead."

She regarded him with surprise and a little bit of apprehension. "As you wish." She rang for their coats and hats and led him out into the small plot of garden behind the house. It was hardly worthy of the name, really, as it was only a square the size of the house itself, walled in from its identical neighbors. But she took Wellborne's arm and they solemnly walked its length.

"Have you heard from your uncle lately, Miss Mont-gomery?" he asked at last.

"No, I have not. I am afraid he does not have much time for writing social letters. I have had a letter from my aunt, and she seems much worried. The political situation, as you know, is worrisome and is beginning to tell on his health."

"I have recently been thinking of beginning a career in politics," he said.

"Indeed? How interesting. I suppose you would run for a seat in Scarborough?"

He flushed slightly. "I am not so ambitious as that. I had only hoped to get my start in political circles. Sophia was shocked when I told her. But it is a better career than gambling." He laughed without humor. "Our father was a great one for the tables."

They walked on in silence for a moment. "I am sorry. It has undone many more families than I would like to think. But I am pleased that you have decided on a more suitable alternative. Your grandmother is pleased?"

"Uh . . . yes. She . . . she is quite pleased. Says she can die in peace now."

Athena remembered that the woman was not well, and regretted mentioning her, since Charles seemed uncomfortable. He did not seemed disposed to talk. It mystified her that he had come for a visit at all, since he knew that Auntie Montie was not overly welcoming when it came to her nieces' callers. In any case, he had picked the worst possible time. She was still reeling from the discovery of that damnable list of names and now to have her sister insisting that she intended to marry the man! It did not bear thinking of. The thought of Cass at the altar with a man like Solage . . . The now-familiar pain under her ribs intensified.

Mr. Wellborne had begun speaking during her reverie.

"You are so clever, Miss Montgomery. It seems as though the London political scene would suit you to the ground. Have you never considered a career as a political wife?"

She looked up at him in surprise. "A political wife?" she echoed blankly. "No. I had not. I might enjoy collecting up-and-coming new politicians for my salon, but I never gave it much thought. I would much rather surround myself with literary people. Besides"—she frowned—"I have no intention of marrying."

He stopped and turned to face her. Somehow the hand she had rested lightly on his arm had become entrapped between his own. "You wound me," he said quietly. "I had hoped that you would consent to marry me."

She blinked up at him. "What?" She must have misheard him. The sharp wind was rebuffed by the high walls of the garden, but her ears were stinging with the cold.

"You must know that I have admired you from the first time I met you at the Upper Rooms. You are so serious, so dignified. I admire your intelligence and I thought . . . that is, I had hoped that you shared my feelings of regard. Surely you are not surprised by my declaration, Miss Montgomery." He smiled gently.

She felt herself go quite warm despite the wind. "I— that is—I don't know—I am very surprised indeed—I never intended . . ." She felt a little dizzy and longed to run back into the house. This could not be right. Charles Wellborne? She could be married to Charles Wellborne. It would most likely be the only chance she would have to be married.

"Athena." His voice was coaxing. In the moment that she looked up at him, perplexed, he kissed her. She started back instantly, and he let her go. "I am sorry. Forgive me, my dear. I was overwhelmed." He didn't look very sorry.

"Please, Mr. Wellborne." She took another step back.

"I regret that I must decline your most—most flattering offer." She clutched her cold hands to her chest. "I am afraid that I was not meant to be married." She smiled weakly. "But it was very kind of you to suggest it."

He advanced upon her. "I did not know that I had taken you so much by surprise. I assumed you knew my feelings, but I can see that you are far too modest to have known my admiration for you. And I understand that it is customary to refuse a suitor at the first request anyway. Do not feel as though you have to make a decision now, Athena." He captured her hands again.

"You misunderstand, sir. It is not surprise that makes me refuse your offer." She whipped her hands out of his and clasped them behind her back. "I do not wish to be married at all." She had been kissed. For the first time in her life. Very well, it was hard to see what all the fuss was about.

His face fell slightly. "But, my dear, only think of what a good match we would make. As a married woman you will enjoy much more freedom. You will no longer have to play companion to your aunt, who, I am sorry to say, does not appreciate you nearly enough. With your political connections, we can move in the highest circles." His voice trailed off.

"Thank you, but I am afraid my answer is still no," she said regretfully. "Shall we go back into the house?"

He nodded, his forehead creased in a slight frown. He did not remove his coat when they entered the house, but collected his umbrella and gloves and continued toward the front door. He allowed the butler to open the door, but then paused. "My offer still stands, Athena," he said softly. "I hope that you will reconsider it."

She did reconsider it. She reconsidered it several times. Marriage to Wellborne would mean a security she had never known. She would no longer be dependent on her parents or Auntie Montie for a roof over her head. She would no longer have to hope that Cass's future husband—perhaps Monsieur Solage!—would allow his maiden sister-in-law to rattle about his house when she got old. She might even have children. Her throat tightened, and she was forced to stare hard out the window of the carriage that conveyed her with Cassiopeia to the assembly at the Upper Rooms.

But no. She did not love Charles. It was ridiculous that she did not, since he was everything amiable, and suited her own rather serious disposition very well. He was not outrageously flirtatious and patently insincere like Monsieur Solage. He was not disturbingly sensual. She forced her thoughts back to the matter at hand. No, Charles would not suit her and that was that.

"Good heavens, Athena! You haven't spoken a word since we left the house!" Cass whispered. "You aren't still cross with me are you?"

"No, of course not. I am just distracted. You look very pretty tonight, Cass. Yellow suits you. What a pity I am too sallow to wear it."

Cass caressed the skirts of the diaphanous overdress. "Nonsense. You would look very well in it. But you insist on wearing such dowdy things. I had great hopes when you bought that bonnet, but—" Her hand stilled suddenly. "Merciful heavens! There is Monsieur Solage! He is doubtlessly going to the assembly, and I shall see him. How will I ever face him?" She ducked down in the carriage as it rolled to a stop in front of the Upper Rooms. Monsieur Solage was indeed walking up the sidewalk in their direction.

"Get up off the floor, you goose! I would advise that you act as naturally as possible and try to forget the whole incident. If he presses you, you should tell the truth, but I would not go and confess the entire story to him for no reason. Most likely he is happy enough to forget it as a trifling incident.''

Cass sighed and righted herself. ''You are right of course. I will have to be especially charming. This marriage scheme is much harder than I thought it would be.'' She frowned and reluctantly climbed out of the carriage after her sister.

''You have arrived at last; now the evening can begin,'' Charles said with a smile as he bowed over Athena's hand. ''Sophia is dancing, but I refused to ask anyone until I could first dance with you.''

''You are very kind, Mr. Wellborne, but I do not intend to dance tonight. I am playing chaperone, if you recall.'' She withdrew her hand, since he showed no apparent inclination to release it. He greeted Cass with little interest and stood silently as a young man approached to solicit Athena's permission to dance with her sister.

As Cass floated off to join the set, Charles frowned slightly. ''I find it ridiculous that you have relegated yourself to the post of chaperone. You are far too young and beautiful.''

''I believe we have had this conversation numerous times. However, if my mother saw fit to allow me to chaperone Cassiopeia, I must certainly be appropriate,'' she replied coolly. She turned to watch the dancers and hoped that he would not continue the conversation. Monsieur Solage had entered the room and stood near the doorway, scanning the crowd. As always, he looked faintly exotic with his dark indigo coat, over a richly embroidered waistcoat and cream satin knee breeches. She dragged her eyes away from him and stared into the crowd.

''Then I must be content to stand by you in your duenna duties. Indeed, it is a much better proposition than dancing, for I shall be able to converse with you all evening without interruption.'' Charles smiled down at her, his blue eyes affectionate.

Athena repressed an urge to find an acquaintance across the room and race off to greet her.

''Athena''—he lowered his voice—''dare I hope that you have reconsidered my suit?''

She clasped her gloved hands and twisted them. ''No, well, that is, yes, I have given it a good deal of thought, and I am afraid that my answer must still be no. Please''— she looked up at him pleadingly—''do not make this more painful for both of us by mentioning it again.'' Solage had seen them and was making his way across the floor to where they stood at the top of the room. She inched away from the fire blazing in the hearth, as the room seemed to have become very airless.

''But you must at least give me leave to hope, my dearest,'' Charles was continuing. ''As my wife you would be a perfectly acceptable chaperone for your sister, if that is what is worrying you.''

''No,'' she snapped, the blood racing through her veins in a sudden wash of terror. She forced herself to speak more kindly. ''Please accept that that must be my answer.''

Solage had reached them.

''Miss Montgomery, Mr. Wellborne, how pleasant to find you here.'' He bowed over her hand and smiled. She was wearing that dowdy gray gown, most likely thinking that it would make her look more like the chaperone she pretended to be. She was too vibrant, too clever to be spending her time sitting along the walls of assembly rooms, watching her sister dance.

''Solage.'' Charles Wellborne sketched a bow and frowned. He obviously felt as though he had staked his claim for the evening.

Dominic returned the man's scowl with a benign smile.

"And where is the lovely Miss . . . Wellborne?" He paused infinitesimally just to make Wellborne sweat. An even deeper expression of displeasure crossed the young man's handsome face.

"She is dancing," he answered gruffly, nodding toward the floor.

Dominic raised his quizzing glass and lazily scanned the room. He felt Wellborne shifting uncomfortably beside him. There was a long silence, broken only by Miss Montgomery occasionally uttering the enthusiastic word "So!" in order to try to touch the whip to the conversation. He heard her sigh faintly in relief when Mrs. Beetling approached.

"Monsieur Solage! You have arrived! How very fortunate. I was hoping that you would, as Celia and I were just wondering aloud to each other how you enjoyed your trip to London. We were just exclaiming—"

"Mrs. Beetling"—he cut her off with a smile—"I was just thinking how pleasant it would be to lead your daughter out to dance"—he bowed slightly in response to her gratified tittering—"but unfortunately I have elected not to dance tonight. I feel certain, however, that Mr. Wellborne will be delighted to do the honor which I am lamentably obliged to forgo." He forced his lips into a serene line at the sight of both Mrs. Beetling's and Mr. Wellborne's discomposure.

Wellborne gave a stiff bow. "I would be honored indeed if Miss Beetling would consent to a dance."

Dominic allowed his mouth to relax into a grin as they withdrew, defeated. "A double rout!" he murmured, flicking a glance at Miss Montgomery. She had been smiling, but she composed her pretty mouth into a frown when she saw his expression.

"I tremble," she replied tartly. "For surely I am the next to be attacked."

"No indeed, Miss Montgomery. For it was you I wished to see tonight." He watched the color rise in her cheeks and smiled. She was shockingly easy to please, and she fought it so hard. She was like a girl fresh from the schoolroom, with all the intelligence and wit of a creature of the highest literary circles.

"Cut line, Solage," she snapped. "I have no patience with your teasing tonight."

"You think that I am merely flattering you?" He took her hand and pressed it, laughing when she whipped it away. "But no, other young ladies I flatter, but you, you are far too serious to merit anything more than the most sincere admiration." She *was* too serious. That was what was so enjoyable about teasing her. He accepted her glowering frown with perfect serenity.

She cleared her throat. "Cass has finished dancing, I see. Perhaps you would like to solicit her for the next one?"

"Indeed I would not. While I am happy to help the poor Miss Cassiopeia when she is helpless and lost, I am here to see you, not your sister."

She chose to ignore this last part. "You were very kind to help her."

"Especially when she schemed so carefully that I should have no choice but to aid her." He grinned at her. Miss Montgomery must know of her sister's adventures. He watched the expression of acute embarrassment cross her face as she compressed her lips.

"She is very sorry for what she did," she said at last. "Please don't mention it to her. She would be mortified. She will not throw herself at you again, I assure you."

He shrugged negligently. "It is nothing. You may make it up to me by dancing with me, Miss Montgomery." His conscience was jabbing him with her uncle's name, but he ignored it.

"I cannot. I have already refused Mr. Wellborne, and you have already told Mrs. Beetling that you would not. Besides, I am not dancing tonight, as I am chaperoning my sister."

"I must protest. You never dance. Do you not like it?"

"Oh no, I like it very much indeed, it is just that—" She broke off lamely as she watched the dancers with a wistful expression.

"Someday you will not be playing chaperone, and that day you must promise that you will dance with me." He smiled warmly. "Are we agreed?"

She nodded, but he realized it was only to pacify him. Miss Montgomery could always be depended on to squash his hopes. Castlereagh, he reminded himself. He turned to watch her sister as she turned gracefully on the arm of Charles Wellborne. "Your sister dances now with Mr. Wellborne," he said quietly, his voice carefully neutral.

"You do not like Charles."

"Charles?" He did not turn to her. "I did not know that you were on such intimate terms, you and . . . Charles."

"He has been very kind to my sister and me," she said repressively. Wellborne and Miss Cassiopeia had joined a set at the far end of the room. They talked avidly as they moved through the figures of the dance; both of them were obviously enjoying themselves.

"Yes," he said slowly, as he watched the laughing couple. "The mysterious Wellbornes."

"Mysterious!" Her eyes opened in surprise. "Pray tell what is mysterious about them?"

He regretted having said anything, but she might as well be on her guard. "They have sprung up full-grown in the middle of Bath." He laughed softly. "Much like how the goddess Athena sprang full-grown from her father's head."

Her pale brown brows drew closer together. "I don't

know what you are talking about," she said impatiently.
"That is, I know the myth, of course. But I fail to see
how it relates to the Wellbornes."

"They are not from Scarborough. They are not from
anywhere. The grandmother they live with does not
exist." He watched her to judge her reaction. The dark
lashes that fringed those gray eyes fluttered slightly, but
she rallied.

"Nonsense," she said firmly. He noticed that she was
pinching the ends of her gloves rather tightly.

"I have said too much. I am sorry," he said gravely.
"I should have been more circumspect, and I have no proof
for my wild accusations." How unfair of him to have even
set the suspicion in her mind. But of course, better now
than later . . . He took her hand and pressed it. "I only wish
for you to be careful." He looked out on to the dance floor.
"And for your sister to be careful. I would not like for her
to be seduced by Wellborne's charm."

She snatched her hand away and clutched it to her body.
Her chin rose slightly. "I received a very flattering offer
from Mr. Wellborne this afternoon." Her eyes dared him
to react.

"Did you indeed?" He tried to sound bored. "Should
I wish you happiness?" He forced his heartbeat to slow.
This could change everything. She could not have
accepted. Not Wellborne.

She shot him an annoyed look. "No. I have no intention
of marrying him."

He relaxed. There was still time. "Then you should
wish me happiness." He tried to pretend that it was only
keeping her away from Wellborne that he cared about.

"I don't know what you are talking about, Monsieur
Solage," she said pettishly.

"For now I can continue to pursue you." If she had
not been born with a truly remarkably beautiful sister,

she would not have been eclipsed. She would have had her own collection of beaux.

Two spots of fury appeared on Athena's cheeks. "First you insult my friends and now you insult me."

"I love to make you angry." He smiled languidly. "The English anger is so fascinating. It is all hissing and no shouting. You have so much restraint. I see now that you long to slap me, but you do not. Such tightly reined passion holds so much promise." He stepped over so that he was blocking her from view from the rest of the room. He saw her expression of anger rise to one of startled anxiety. He reached up one hand to caress her forearm above the elbow-length gloves she wore. Such fine white skin. She jerked back as though he had burned her. "I would love to see your passion unleashed," he continued softly.

"Step away from me this instant. You are making a scene," she said coolly.

"Hiss hiss." He laughed and moved away. "Athena"— he gave the word a caress—"you are the goddess of prudence and wisdom, but I sometimes forget that you are the goddess of warfare as well. And warfare is all about passion." Her expression of fury pleased him. He cast a glance over his shoulder in the direction of Wellborne. "Tell your Paris that I am laying siege to Athens."

He was very nearly out of hearing before she could collect herself enough to call out after him, "You are mixing your stories, Monsieur Solage. Paris and Helen were besieged at Troy, not Athens." He thought for a moment that she would run after him and give him a lecture on Greek history. He grinned. She was a bluestocking to the last.

Chapter Ten

"Insufferable!"

"What?" Cass asked sleepily, her head lolling on the carriage's squabs. "Who?"

"Solage!"

"Solage?" she repeated in surprise. "But, Athena! Everyone was talking about how you had caught his eye! You spoke nearly the whole evening and he didn't dance with anyone because you were not dancing. Everyone is saying that he is your conquest. Athena's Conquest. It does sound rather literary. I thought you might like it."

Athena gave a derisive snort.

"Well he was certainly staring deeply and longingly into your eyes." Cass laughed.

"Yes, as he insulted me," she returned acidly. "I know he is your beau, Cass, but I must say I think he is very bad *ton*. Perhaps such bold conduct is acceptable on the Continent, but it will not fly in Bath, I can tell you that. I hope you do not intend to encourage him." She felt her cheeks warm again at the memory of his hand caressing her arm.

"My beau?" Her sister gave another sleepy laugh. "Indeed, I gave him up hours ago. I have decided not to marry him after all. I would rather a man who is more serious, more sincere. Like your Charles. He was very kind to me tonight, you know. Generally I find him dull and a little sanctimonious, but quite enjoyed being with him tonight."

Athena felt like screaming. Instead she said calmly, "How silly you are, Cass. There is nothing but friendship between Charles Wellborne and myself. But I do think that you would do well to encourage more men of his ilk. You have no need of these flirtatious rakes who have no serious intentions."

"No indeed," Cass agreed cheerfully. She leaned her head back with a smile and closed her eyes.

Athena watched her sister carefully. Hopefully Cass was safe from Solage. The last thing they needed was for her sister to be throwing herself after . . . well, could he be a spy? He was dangerous indeed, but it was not for political reasons. She braced herself in her seat as they began the ascent up the hill to the Crescent.

It was impossible that he should be a spy. Surely he would look more furtive. He could not appear in public looking so handsome and relaxed and be able to greet her, his enemy's niece, with such civility. But perhaps there had been a predatory look in his dark eyes. Perhaps he enjoyed the perverse irony of his standing as special friend of the Montgomery family. Her eyes flicked back to Cass. Perhaps he intended to seduce Castlereagh's niece, just as the Battford sisters had suggested. But then why did he not take advantage of her role as the lost innocent the other day? Was she herself to be the victim of his revenge? She smiled at the Gothic phrasing of her own thoughts.

Her mind dragged back to their conversation. He had warned her about the Wellbornes. It was probably some petty jealousy, but his words were worrying. Was everyone around her not what they claimed to be? She was not a fanciful woman. She was not prone to dramatization or imaginings. How was it that she was now faced with a possible spy who now claimed that her new friends in Bath were frauds. It was patently ridiculous.

By the time the footman had opened the carriage door in front of the house on Royal Crescent, she had made up her mind. She would go with Sophia to find out for herself. If Solage had nothing to hide, Falk would tell them so. If he did have something to hide, well, she owed it to her uncle to divine what it was. She had to find out why he had that list.

"Well?" Sophia's brows rose encouragingly.

"Well what?" Athena closed the door to the drawing room, rang for tea, and went to sit down beside her friend.

"What did you find out?"

"When? What are you talking about?"

"Last night!" Sophia laughed incredulously. "You had the entire assembly room on their ear by talking half the night with the mysterious Monsieur Solage. He has been dubbed Athena's Conquest."

"Society's sarcasm is very witty," she said dryly, ignoring the sudden feeling of heat in the room. "I am surprised that anyone noticed. I also spoke with yourself, Mrs. Beetling, and your brother. Does anyone care about that?"

Sophia smiled wickedly. "My brother is not a spy."

"I am convinced that no one is a spy. The entire notion

is ridiculous.'' The tea tray arrived, so she could not continue, but she cast Sophia an expressive look while the servant set down the dishes.

"He will be out of the house next Wednesday," her friend continued when Betty had left the room. "That is the day he rides to London. He has done so every week since he arrived. We can enter the house and search his chambers then."

Athena set down the teapot so suddenly that the lid rattled and tea splashed out of the spout. "Are you mad?" She dabbed ineffectually at the amber stain on the white tea mat.

"I will die if I don't know the truth. Besides, we owe it to England."

Athena gave a scornful snort. "I am not sure England will see it that way when we are put on the dock for housebreaking." She stirred her tea meditatively. "He was horridly bold last night, Sophie. Nothing would please me more than to bring him down a peg."

"And this is the perfect way to do it. He thinks you are completely under his thumb, when actually, you were allaying his suspicions so that you could do some reconnaissance work."

"Was I?" She laughed. "Oh yes, that's right, I was." She sipped the tea, but it burned her mouth. "I think that I will just tell my uncle about the list and let him decide how to handle things."

Sophia looked shocked. "No! Oh, Athena, you can't! Leave everything to a man? Your mother would be ashamed. We are resourceful women, and we can figure this out for ourselves. Just think of how grand it will be to be able to present to your uncle the whole plot."

"I doubt there is a plot."

"Then if you tell him about the list without looking in Solage's rooms, you will be worrying him for nothing.

If we find nothing, you may tell your uncle or not, however you see fit.'' She cast Athena a pleading look.

"All right,'' she said at last. "But only because he was toying with me last night. He must think that I am terribly naïve to fall for a lingering glance and neatly turned innuendo.'' She shrugged, silently fearing that she was indeed terribly naïve.

"Leave everything to me. I will have Charles escort me here for a visit after you go with your aunt to the Pump Room on Wednesday morning. I will tell him that I intend to spend the day here. We'll tell your aunt that we are going out somewhere. I will let you make up an excuse.''

"Thank you,'' she murmured. "I am not at all sure that this is a good idea. You will ruin my reputation as a straitlaced old spinster.''

"Fiddle!'' Sophia exclaimed. "Now, I will run along and work out the details.'' She stood up. "Don't forget; Wednesday morning.''

Athena helped her collect her pelisse, bonnet, and maid, and bid her good-bye at the door before she went upstairs to her aunt.

The old woman's mental state was indicated by the shawl flung nearly to the middle of the room. Athena picked it up and folded it.

"Those Wellbornes run tame around here!'' she exclaimed pettishly, plucking at another shawl around her shoulders. "You girls think that you own this house with your visitors coming and going at all hours. There isn't a minute of daylight that there isn't one or the other of that havey-cavey pair about the place.''

"I am sorry. I know you dislike visitors,'' Athena said soothingly. "But this is only the second time this week that Sophia has called.

"And her brother is walking this minute with your

sister in the garden!'' her aunt said accusingly. ''And he
was here yesterday walking in the garden with *you!*'' she
finished triumphantly.

Athena started. How peculiar that he had not asked to
see her. Perhaps he knew that Sophia was with her and
did not wish to disturb them. It seemed rather odd that
he would not have escorted his sister home. She moved
to the window and looked out. Cass and Charles were
walking the graveled perimeter of the garden. Athena
shrugged. ''I will ask him not to come around if it dis-
pleases you,'' she said calmly. ''But I rather suspect that
you enjoy thinking up rather scandalous reasons why
everyone comes to visit.'' She smiled at her aunt and
returned to the chair beside the old woman's settee.

''There is only one reason men come to visit: your
sister,'' Auntie Montie replied sharply. ''The sooner we
have married her off, the sooner our lives can return to
normal. I thought that old stick Charles Wellborne was
dangling after you, Athena, but it looks as though he's
decided to try for Cassiopeia instead. I won't countenance
the match. Not with either of you. There is something
havey-cavey about those two. You are too clever to be
taken by his shamery, but I daresay your sister might be.
Between Wellborne and that damned charming Frenchman, we'll be lucky if Cassiopeia doesn't end up entirely
in the soup.'' She laughed as though this were very funny.
''Now run downstairs and tell your sister that I need her
here. I don't of course, but that Puritan will have to take
a hint and leave.''

Athena reluctantly complied. She wondered, as she
descended the stairs, how her aunt could disapprove of
one of Cass's suitors because he was too dull and the
other because he was too charming. Were they Cass's
suitors or were they her own? She pressed her hand to

her forehead to forcibly smooth it. Things were getting very complicated.

Taking a shawl from a peg by the door, she went outside to retrieve the couple. They were sitting on a low wooden bench with their backs to her as they watched a pair of swallows build their nest in a tree on the other side of the garden wall. Athena's slippers made no noise on the grass as she crossed to them.

"But, my darling," Charles was saying, "you cannot be surprised by my offer. You must know that I have loved you from afar since I first met you at the assembly rooms. Your vivacity and good nature have inspired my admiration even more than your beauty, Miss Cassiopeia. Tell me I might hope!"

He continued to speak, but Athena retreated out of hearing. Her ears were ringing. She turned away just as she saw him fervently clasp Cass's hand and bring it to his heart. "Cass!" she shouted, praying her voice did not tremble "There you are! Auntie wants you this moment." She clenched her jaw as Cass leapt guiltily to her feet.

"Thank you very much for visiting, Mr. Wellborne." Her sister gasped, extending her fingers to shake his hand and then whipping them back before he could respond. "Good-bye." She turned on her heel and ran into the house.

Athena listened to her sister's footsteps crunch away on the crushed gravel path. She raised her eyes to Charles and saw that he was regarding her warily. "Mr. Wellborne," she said at last, "how kind of you to come to visit us. I regret that my aunt is not well enough for us to receive you any longer today. But thank you so much for coming." She smiled enough to split her cheeks.

"Athena, I had hoped to have a word with you," he began gently with a look that she was beginning to think of as overly genuine in his eyes.

"I'm so sorry, Charles," she cut him off. "Today is the worst of all times. Auntie is very cross and, to tell you the truth, I am quite out of humor myself." She ushered him through the house, shook his hand firmly, and shut the front door behind him with a very forceful hand.

Chapter Eleven

"There he is."

"Who?" Athena looked around the Pump Room, a tingling rush of panic pulsing through her.

"Lord Falk," Auntie Montie replied with a scowl. "That old windbag. He is always staring at me." She pulled her shawl more tightly around her shoulders and sniffed.

Athena smiled. The old man was indeed staring very hard at them. His white hair floated out in cloudlike wisps from his shining head. He would have looked like a benevolent old warlock if his brows had not stuck out to such alarming lengths. He glowered at them and motioned them over impatiently. "Shall I push you over there? Do you wish to speak to him?"

"I should say not! I have not spoken to him in twenty years. Why should I start today? Wheel me to face the other way. I can't stand someone who stares so impertinently." She gestured for her niece to push the chair toward the other end of the room. "He made me an offer of marriage you know," Auntie Montie said suddenly.

"Lord Falk?" Athena gasped.

Her aunt laughed her dry, cracking laugh. "You needn't sound so surprised, missy. Twenty years ago, I could still get up and dance the Scotch reel with the rest of 'em."

"I don't doubt it, madam. It is just that I had no idea that you even knew Lord Falk."

"He said he was making me an offer I could not refuse." She laughed again. It sounded a bit like joints popping. "So I refused him."

"And you have not spoken to him since?"

"Not a word. But that does not stop him from staring at me like a fool. He might be a wonder in Parliament, but here in Bath he looks the veriest gapeseed." Athena could have sworn that Auntie Montie giggled. "Speaking of gapeseeds, what is wrong with that sister of yours?

"I don't know what you mean. She never wishes to go this early to the Pump Room. I hardly thought that you would be surprised if she did not wish to accompany us today."

"Not just this morning. The girl is in a high state of the fidgets. She's got a flea in her chemise over something. Now don't you gasp at me, Athena Montgomery. We weren't nearly so puritanical in my day. If you are going to get all-over blushy about the word chemise, perhaps you should just marry that dull dog Wellborne and be done with it." She sniffed. "I want to go home." She gave regal wave of her hand. "Push me to the door. Andrew is waiting outside to push me up the hill."

Athena was about to protest that she could have managed the Bath chair up the hill without the help of the footman, when she saw Charles and Sophia crossing the court of the Abbey Church. Her fingers clenched anxiously. She had somehow hoped that something would happen to prevent their embarking on this ridiculous, and highly illegal escapade. And then to have to see Charles again after what had happened the other day! She was glad that Cass had elected to stay at home.

"How fortunate that you are here. I was just going up to visit you." Sophia's eyes darted to Auntie Montie. Athena was standing behind the wheeled chair and could not see her aunt's expression, but it doubtlessly plainly showed her opinion of their proposed visit. "But I have a better idea. Perhaps Charles could see your aunt home, and you and I could have a nice coze while we look for that pair of gloves I was telling you about in the shop on Bond Street." She smiled serenely. What a cool liar Sophia was, Athena thought with some admiration.

Auntie Montie craned her neck around and looked at Athena. "Well," she said in a completely audible tone, "if it will keep them out of my house, maybe you had better go with her. Buy yourself some new gloves too. You could be a good deal prettier than your sister if you would just put yourself out a little more and stop playing the dowd."

Athena smiled stiffly. Of all things to say in public—and in front of Charles Wellborne too. He had obviously decided he preferred Cass's charms to her own, gloves or no gloves. She reminded herself firmly that she had rejected Charles's offer, and he was therefore free to pursue anyone he wanted. "If you don't mind Mr. Wellborne seeing you home, I would be happy to shop for a little while with Sophia."

"Pooh, I don't need anyone to see me home. I have Andrew."

"I insist, Miss Montgomery." Charles bowed politely to Auntie Montie.

"Yes, I imagined you would. But if you are thinking I will let you in the house so that you can rendezvous with my niece—either niece for that matter. You had better rethink you thoughts.''

Charles accepted this threat with equanimity and the strange trio set off up the street toward the Royal Crescent.

''How marvelous! Everything is working out even better than we had planned.'' Sophia clapped her hands.

''We have not done anything yet,'' Athena reminded her dolefully. She cast a look around them to make sure that Lord Falk was not lurking anywhere nearby, and began to walk toward his house on Rivers Street. It was cool, but the uphill walk made her uncomfortably warm underneath her gray pelisse. ''Sophia, I am not at all pleased with this. What are we to do, ring the door and deal with that deaf old butler again?''

''Nonsense. You need to learn to have a little fun in life. You are a good deal too serious. What a grand adventure this is!'' She flung her arms out expressively. ''We will sneak in the kitchen door and slip up to Solage's rooms. It will not take longer than a moment. We will be out in a quarter of an hour. Surely Falk's other servants are as old and deaf as the butler. It will be frightfully easy.''

Athena stifled her feelings of foreboding. Perhaps she *was* too serious. How refreshing it would be to shuffle off the eternal feelings of responsibility and have a lark. As she looked up at the imposing white front of the house ornamented with ponderously graceful stone baroque flourishes, she was not sure that now was the time. They loitered in the street, examining the building. Like every other house on the street, an iron fence surrounded the kitchen courtyard. There was no sign of life.

''I hadn't remembered that the area railing was so high.'' Sophia eyed it doubtfully. ''I don't think that we could climb over it without causing a scene. Perhaps we could go around by the mews . . .''

Athena reminded herself of the evening in the Upper Rooms. Solage obviously thought that she was a dull prude who was easily overset by London flirtatiousness and Continental banter. She marched up to the door and turned the handle. "I declare, Sophia. You make things much too difficult." She smiled, opened the door, and politely gestured that Sophia should enter first.

Her friend regarded her with an expression of admiration. "Unlocked! It isn't very dramatic, but it is certainly easier," she whispered with a grin.

The hallway was nearly as cold as it was outside, but very still after the wind blowing down Rivers Street. It was silent except for the faint rhythmic banging of a window somewhere on the floor. Athena looked at her friend with some trepidation. Now what? Sophia put a finger to her lips and crept silently up the main staircase. A chambermaid was singing softly to herself in one of the rooms. From the clatter, it sounded as though she were cleaning the hearth in one of the several receiving rooms. Sophia led the way to the second set of stairs. As they continued deeper into the house, Athena felt her palms grow damper. In the foyer, it might have been easy to explain their presence. Couldn't they have somehow walked into the wrong house? Now they were slinking along the hallway leading to bedchambers. Housebreaking in the middle of the day—her knees trembled uncomfortably.

"Which one?" Sophia mouthed the words, indicating an array of doors lining the hallway.

Athena shrugged irritably. What a stupid plan. What were they thinking? She thought of Dominic's veiled expression as he had insolently rubbed his palm up her arm in front of the entire assembly. He obviously thought she would fall into his arms like a rag doll. Yes, a man like that probably did have something to hide. She walked to the nearest door and opened it. It was empty. "Start at the other end of the hall," she whispered to Sophia. "Look for a guest room that is obviously occupied. Don't do the one at the end—it is most likely to be Lord Falk's rooms." Galvanized, she tried several other rooms. The maids seemed be finished here. At last she found what she was looking for. In a pretty, bright room she saw his coat lying on the bed. Just seeing it made her skin jump. She drew a breath and then leaned back out the door to motion frantically to Sophia.

She closed the bedroom door behind them. "All right. Where do we look?" She tried to speak in a normal voice, but it sounded hoarse and frightened.

"I'll start at the desk and you look through the books." She indicated a crate of books that sat on the floor near the desk. "You found the list in one of his books; he may have hidden other information in them." Sophia's eyes sparkled in anticipation. She began methodically disassembling the neat dockets of papers stacked there. Athena watched her for a moment, surprised at the change in her friend. She showed no compunction about reading everything she came across. Oh well, that was what they were there for, wasn't it?

She gave herself a shake and knelt down beside the crate of books. Most were French authors she did not know. Gingerly she opened each one and shook it, looking to see if papers fell out. The clock on the mantel clicked steadily as she piled the books one by one. At last she reached the bottom of the crate. "Sophia, this is ridiculous. I have found nothing but a list of things to do dated November of 1813. Please let us forget this and slip out while we still can." She began putting the books back, hoping that Dominic remembered their order no better than she.

"Just a moment," Sophia whispered urgently.

"Have you found something?"

"I am not sure. Mostly there are letters. My French is not very good, so I don't understand them too well. Perhaps he was using code words to make it look like ordinary correspondences." She looked up from the letter she was frowning at. "You are fluent in French—read these. No better yet, we will take them with us."

"No, we couldn't! He would be sure to notice."

"Indeed I would."

They both looked up in horror. Silent as a cat, Dominic Solage had slipped into the room and was standing with his back to the door, regarding them with narrowed eyes.

Chapter Twelve

Athena scrambled to her feet and looked around wildly for a place to flee. She was vaguely aware that Sophia had risen so quickly that the chair she was sitting on fell backward to the floor with a clatter.

"Mesdamoiselles, if I had known I was to be entertaining you, I would have been here when you arrived." The outside halves of his brows rose sarcastically.

"Monsieur Solage—" Athena found that she could still speak only in a whisper. "It is not what you think—that is—well . . ." she trailed off helplessly. Did the door at the end of the room lead out or only to a dressing room?

"Only a dressing room, I'm afraid," he replied, as though he could read her mind. "Now, Miss Montgomery, Miss Wellborne, to what do I owe the honor of this little visit?" He crossed the room and sat down gracefully in one of the chairs facing the hearth. "Oh dear, and no fire. You must have been freezing. I would ring for the maid, but I am afraid that, despite the fact that there are two of you, it would compromise both of your reputations irrevocably.'' A smile dragged at one side of his mouth. ''However much it might improve mine.''

Athena longed to strangle him. ''Then we will leave immediately,'' she replied, her voice clipped. She stepped toward the door, only to wince as she saw the gaping keyhole.

Dominic held up the key with a Gallic shrug. ''In a moment. First, I would very much like an answer to my question.''

''We know everything, Solage,'' Sophia said brazenly. ''And what's more, Charles knows, too, so if you have any plans to kidnap us or kill us, he will find, make no mistake.''

The ends of his brows rose again. It made him look a bit satanic. ''Ah, the honorable Mr. Charles Wellborne.'' He stroked his chin meditatively. ''He knows everything, too, does he? Well that certainly foils my evil plans. And why did he send over two unprotected women, brave and resourceful though they doubtlessly are, to do the reconnaissance work?'' There was a dangerous glitter in his dark eyes.

''I'm warning you, Solage, my brother is waiting for us in the street. If we do not reappear in two minutes, he will come in after us.'' Sophia clenched her hands into fists and advanced on him aggressively. Athena watched the exchange between the two with surprised fascination. She felt as though she were at a play. There was a subtext between them that she somehow did not feel a part of.

He made a dramatically helpless gesture. ''Forget about Charles for the moment.'' He spoke the *Ch* of the name in a very foreign manner. ''I am all adrift. Please do explain to me why you are here, and what it is that you know all about that I would perhaps be tempted to kill you for, Miss deWit?''

Sophia blanched but held her ground. ''You are a French spy. You are passing information on to Napoleon. The only reason you are doing the pretty to the Montgomerys is because of their relationship to Castlereagh.'' She stepped up so close to Dominic that Athena inadvertently drew back for him. He continued to regard her calmly from his seat by the hearth. ''I can call the watch right now, Monsieur Solage,'' she continued. ''Miss Montgomery and I would be regarded as heroines.''

''And your brother who is waiting outside, of course,'' he added helpfully.

She ignored him. ''You will be hung for a traitor.''

''Or simply deported.'' He shrugged again. ''Who knows? But I am curious, Miss deWit, why you do not simply call the watch this moment. Why are you speaking in the future tense? Are you hoping that I will make you a counteroffer to your generous suggestion that I be offered up to the authorities as a spy?''

''Good heavens!'' Athena interjected. ''You are both being ridiculous. I cannot believe I am hearing such Gothic rubbish.'' She folded her hands awkwardly ''Monsieur Solage. I am afraid that I let my imagination run away with me.''

''I would never have dreamed that you had such a fault,'' he murmured, turning his glittering dark eyes on her. His fury was veiled by politeness, but it was a veil that could be cast off at any moment. ''I always imagined that you were a singularly unimaginative young woman.'' He steepled his fingers together and regarded her with a mild expression that was falsified by a tense grimness about his mouth.

She cringed inwardly, but held her ground, hoping that her face did not betray her. And here she had been thinking she was half in love with the man. She was temporarily distracted from his gross insult by her own mental articulation of that idea. Love? No. She could never have felt that way about the man now sitting in front of her, regarding her with his brows tilted evilly upward in an expression of mocking suspense.

"I . . . apologize, Monsieur Solage," she managed to choke out through clenched teeth. "We had no right to invade the privacy of your rooms. Please forgive our grievous imposition." She clamped her hand to Sophia's elbow to try to staunch any further comments from her. "If you will kindly unlock the door, we will leave you in peace, and I assure you that you will not be troubled with an incident of this kind again."

"Indeed, you are welcome at any time." He rose to his feet and bowed with a facetious gesture. "I would love to show you my secret stash of gunpowder and collection of pilfered orders from your General Wellington. But alas"—he feigned an expression of disconsolance—"I have sent them all off to Emperor Napoleon by this morning's post." He crossed to the door and unlocked it without looking at them.

Sophia started to protest, but Athena gripped her arm tighter and her friend's statement dissolved into a whimper. She started when her own arm was clamped firmly by Dominic's strong fingers as he parted the two of them and escorted them both out of the room with a rather less-than-delicate touch.

Athena was nearly panting as she descended the stairs and crossed the hall at a half run to keep up with his long strides. He threw open the door and looked out with exaggerated dismay.

"But where is Mr. Wellborne? He must have gotten tired of waiting and gone home. How terrible. Shall I call you a chair?"

"No indeed." Athena jerked her arm from his hand. "We will make our own way home." She favored him with a glare of pure loathing and flounced down the steps with Sophia close behind. "What an odious man!" she exclaimed as soon as they were safely around the corner. "He said I have no imagination."

Her friend stared at her. "Athena, he's a spy. He as much as admitted it! If you hadn't gotten your back up and nearly broken my arm in the process, we could have been well on the go! If he thought we were going to go to the authorities he would have offered us any amount of money to keep us quiet."

"What are you talking about?" she replied irritably. "If he actually was a spy . . . one, we would have found something to indicate it instead of a ream of rather boring letters from his sister about her children, and two, he would have killed us or some such thing to keep us from telling, and three, if he didn't kill us, we would have gone to the authorities immediately and not tried extorting money from him." She counted the reasons off on her gloved fingers, and then gestured in frustration. "Where in the world did you get the idea that we should ask for money?"

"It would have been high adventure, Athena! He would have been entirely under our thumb!" Sophia protested. "Now we shall be lucky if we are not arrested ourselves. He would do that, just to be spiteful." She frowned thoughtfully as they walked toward the house on Royal Crescent.

Athena moaned. "That was the most stupid thing I have ever done. I am so ashamed. I cannot believe I talked myself into believing such ridiculous gossip about him." She folded her arms defensively. "And the insolence of that man! I hate him, I truly do." She stomped up the hill in silence for a moment. "And you are right, Sophia.

He most likely has been flirting with Cassiopeia—even me for heaven's sake—and in the most horribly outrageous way, only because of our connection to Castlereagh. Not because he is a spy of course," she amended quickly. "But probably because he is a Whig and is hoping to torture my uncle by making his whole family miserable!" She sniffed violently. How could she possibly have felt anything for that man? A man who thought her uninteresting and unimaginative but enjoyed torturing her in front of the entire assembly at the Upper Rooms probably just to see how poor, plain Miss Montgomery would react to a little flirtation. Oh she positively seethed! "Why did he call you Miss deWit?" she asked suddenly.

"I don't know. The man is obviously insane. We're lucky he didn't murder us." Sophia made an irritated gesture of dismissal.

"I shall turn off here to go home. I will see you soon," she said awkwardly, as they arrived at the corner near Sophia's house. "I am sorry this turned out so badly."

"Good-bye." Sophia nodded coolly.

Athena watched her walk down the street for a moment before she turned to continue up the hill. What a horrid situation. She had offended Sophia by ridiculing her, but good heavens! Had she really thought to embroil them both in some wild blackmail scheme? Even if Solage had been a spy, it was extreme folly. But then, perhaps she was simply too dull, too ordinary to ever contemplate anything more than the prosaic. She frowned at the pavement. It couldn't possibly be a more bleak day. There was nothing in it to even hint that not less than two weeks ago it had been lovely enough for a picnic. She thought of how Dominic had spent the day with her when he could have been in the radiant company of any other woman.

Now he thought of her as something worse than a

common thief. Sophia was insulted that she had not supported her insane scheme, and Charles . . . well Charles had transferred his affection to her sister in less time than it takes for the cat to lick its ear. He preferred someone less serious and more vivacious! She walked the length of the Crescent's lawn twice before she was calm enough to go into the house. She couldn't very well pretend to be a frivolous little butterfly, and she couldn't pretend to be adventurous. People would just have to come to accept that she was plain, ordinary, unexciting, serious, bluestocking Athena Montgomery.

"They were what?" Lord Falk looked stunned.

"They were in my room, looking through my effects," Dominic replied. He paced the room several times before he spoke again. "I myself was shocked. I suspected that the deWits were up to no good, but who would have thought that Athena Montgomery was mixed up in it."

Falk poured them both a drink. "I don't know," he said with a sigh at last. "I find it very disturbing. You are of course aware that this compromised your security. I cannot allow you to courier my comments to the Committee if it cannot be kept quiet." He winced as he propped his gouty leg up in a stool. "Damn, Solage, two chits who have read too many Gothic romances! I could have understood the house being infiltrated by French spies if there *were* any in Bath, and what self-respecting creature, no matter how feather-witted, would suspect spies in Bath of all places. I myself would never have come to this dissolute playground of the decrepit, if it hadn't been for this damn leg of mine. Blast, what were those ninnyhammers thinking? That a city full of batty octogenarians could possibly harbor the country's closest secrets? That a few dull assemblies run by Masters of Ceremonies who think the quadrille daring, never mind the waltz, would be dens of political intrigue? Half of Bath is gouty and the other half is deaf! Deaf I tell you!" His voice rose to a shout.

"I, however, am not," Dominic reminded him with a dry half smile.

Falk made an impatient gesture. "Don't interrupt me in the middle of a rant." He took a sip of his drink and nearly choked on it. "Girls!" he sputtered. "I have to let go the best man I ever worked with because of a couple of lovestruck girls!"

"Miss deWit hoped to find blackmail material. Miss Montgomery—I don't believe she is lovestruck," Dominic muttered. "Carried away, perhaps, but not love. Is hate-struck an expression?"

"No. For the love of Murphy, Solage, learn some English. Your mother would be ashamed. Good Somerset girl she was, and here you are speaking like some damn milliner!"

"Forgive me." Dominic inclined his head slightly. "However, I do wish that you would reconsider, Falk. You cannot get to London every week yourself, and the Bath waters, they appear to be the only thing to help your gout. If you find someone else to courier your letters to the Committee, it will mean taking them into your confidence and trusting that they will either not read the letters or, do as I do: discuss your opinion with the Committee, give my opinion as well, and then tell you what transpired." He compressed his lips and regarded Lord Falk with doubt. "I would regret very much to be excluded from the talks."

"I know, Solage, I know." Falk took another drink and rearranged his leg. "I just can't think of another way." He was silent for a long moment. A log in the hearth broke apart with a loud crack and fell in two halves between the andirons. "Wellbornes, deWits, whatever you wish to call them." He scowled. "Why didn't anyone tell us that the business partner no one ever saw was a woman. Here we were all the time thinking they were brothers."

"And ingratiating themselves with Athena," Dominic said, almost to himself. "I have been very remiss."

"Well, like as not, the deWit girl knows nothing about the Jamaica Isles Company. A pretty little slip of a girl like that couldn't have had a notion in her head. Like as not, it was her brother who invented the scheme."

Dominic eyed his mentor with doubt. He himself would not have been surprised if Sophia had pulled off the entire scheme herself. "The sister offered her silence for money, so I suspect that they are game for anything."

"It's the Montgomery chit I can't figure out."

Dominic stared into the fire for a long moment. "Myself also," he admitted at last. "She seems very simple, the serious woman—bluestocking you say? It is a strange expression. Yes, the bluestocking. She is lonely beneath that cultivated coolness." He pressed his fingers against his lips. "She is being courted by Charles Wellborne. I had hoped to distract her from him."

"I know your style of distraction. Seduction more like." A laugh rumbled in Falk's throat. "Thank God I don't have daughters, Solage. I would be obliged to shoot you."

"Indeed, I would be honored," he replied absently. "I had hoped to do Castlereagh a favor by keeping the Wellbornes away from the Montgomery ladies, but I will now remove myself from the entire affair. If she thinks me a spy, I—*enfin,* I can do nothing to disabuse her." He made a dismissive gesture and stood up. "I wash my hands of her."

"You were the one who involved yourself with the

silly creatures in the first place. Castlereagh never asked you to interfere with his nieces, and he certainly won't thank you. Besides, Louisa Mongomery is an old dragon fierce enough to scare off any potential fortune hunters and adventurers.'' Falk shook his head and took another drink. He reached down and gingerly massaged his toe.

''It's the Committee that has me worried. With Napoleon advancing on Paris and his army growing daily, my presence is of vital importance. I suppose I will just have to drag my carcass up to London myself, much as I hate the place. Nothing else to be done. You will stay here, of course.'' He stopped Dominic's protest with a gesture. ''Nonsense. Whatever your objections are, they are pure nonsense. You will stay here, because to do anything else would cause talk. I will keep you informed as to the Committee and in another week or so, I will have you join me in Town.'' He sighed and hauled himself painfully to his feet. ''I knew this arrangement was too cozy to last. You did me a great service, Dominic, and I thank you. Both my leg and the Committee thank you. But now I am going to have to ask that you step back for a while. All the eyes of Bath will be on you, since there is no way on earth those chits are going to be able to keep their mouths closed about their adventure. I'd lay a monkey that by tomorrow Bath will have word that you have a collection of Wellington's love letters, know who bore Nelson's illegitimate daughter, and are Boney's personal valet!''

Dominic closed his eyes and exhaled wearily. ''Falk, don't exile me here. Let me come with you to London. No one ever notices me there.''

''I'm sorry, Solage.'' Falk shook his head. ''If you leave Bath, it will only start the old tabbies talking. If they scrutinize you, they will scrutinize me and damn it, I can't afford that right now! You'll serve England and

France better by staying still." He took up his silver-headed cane and hobbled to the door. Once there, he turned back with a dry laugh. "It is what you get for being too dashed charming, Solage. I told you you could never be inconspicuous, you old dog." He stumped off muttering, "Trust me to be saddled with a Frenchman. One who women seem to find irresistible. I needed someone who wouldn't be noticed, and I get a man who becomes the talk of Bath."

Chapter Thirteen

"What is wrong with you, Athena?" Auntie Montie snapped irritably. "I have spoken to you twice. You've gone deaf as Lady Glen."

Athena started. "I'm sorry, Auntie. I was not paying attention. Are you ready to leave the Pump Room?"

"Your head is entirely in the clouds. I was asking you to wheel me over to Lord Falk."

"What!" she cried out in horror. "He is here?" A wild look around informed her that he was, and misery of miseries, Solage was with him. He was stooped solicitously over Falk's wheeled Bath chair, and did not look up to see her. Lord Falk, however, was regarding her with open curiosity. He must know. Solage must have told him. Her cheeks burned with shame.

"But, Auntie," she protested, "I thought that you were not on speaking terms with Lord Falk."

The old woman sniffed. "He has been gesturing to me this whole morning, the old fool! I suppose it is about time to patch things up. I'd lay a monkey he is dying and wants to apologize before he cocks up his toes.''

''Perhaps you could just send a note,'' Athena suggested weakly.

''No, you'd better roll me over there. He is becoming quite frantic, and the old imbecile will doubtlessly cause a scene if I don't go see what he wants.''

''I . . . I think that I would like a sample of the water. Cassiopeia will take you to Falk. She is just across the room with Charles and Sophia.''

''Fustian. Get your glass of that nasty water later. Push me, girl!''

Deciding that she was behaving like a coward, Athena drew a deep breath, composed her face into prim neutral lines, and pushed her aunt's chair over to the corner where Lord Falk was gesturing rather urgently.

''Listen here, Louisa, have that chit of yours push you out into the square. It's too damn close in here to breathe, never mind talk.'' He slapped Dominic's coat sleeve and gestured toward the door.

Dominic complied without looking at her. She could see his profile as he maneuvered Falk's chair out of the room. It was positively bulging with tensed muscles.

''Solage, you know Louisa Montgomery and her niece, don't you?'' Falk indicated them with a flap of his hand. ''Then there is no need for introductions. Push us around the square and mind you don't go too fast; bouncing over the cobbles hurts my leg like the very devil.''

''Miss Montgomery, Miss Athena Montgomery.'' Dominic inclined his head slightly toward them before he set out pushing Falk's chair at a sedate pace.

''There now, Athena, slow down,'' Auntie Montie commanded. ''I don't mind the pace, but apparently Old Falk must pander to that leg of his.''

Athena clenched her teeth and stared straight in front

of her. Of all times for her aunt to decided to reconcile with Lord Falk. After twenty years, it had to be today!

"I trust you are well, Miss Montgomery," Solage said coolly. "I hear that Napoleon continues to advance on Paris. You must be kept busy protecting your nation from invasion from across the Channel."

She flicked him a glance of loathing. "I apologized already, sir. If you mean to go to the authorities, by all means do so. I would prefer it to your torturing me with my folly."

He laughed softly, but it was a harsh sound. "But I think I prefer to torture you. After all, it is what we spies are best at." When she remained silent, he continued. "How is Miss Wellborne? I should hate to think that she is missing out on this prime opportunity to share in your humiliation."

"I do not know," she replied shortly. "And you needn't vent your anger on her. The entire debacle was my idea."

"I do not think that it was," he replied, his voice low.

"So you are leaving Bath are you, Gregory?" Auntie Montie's voice rose up in the silence. "Good riddance I say. Now the ladies in London will have to countenance your impertinent stares."

"You're so shortsighted, you can't see your hand in front of your face, never mind me staring at you across the Pump Room, Louisa," Falk countered irritably. "You're as vain as a chit making her first bow. Mind my leg, Solage! You're racing on like we're trying to beat the London Mail. Besides, there ain't anyone of those old bags, in London or here either, worth a second look besides you."

"I see you are attempting to do the pretty," Auntie Montie returned. "Been taking lessons from that French coxcomb of yours?"

Athena turned to Solage. "You have tried to sour my

friendship with the Wellbornes from the first,'' she hissed. ''With all your ridiculous warnings about them. Perhaps they are not the first stare of fashion and perhaps ... perhaps they are not exactly from Scarborough—and just because Auntie does not remember their family does not mean that they are not. But I am certain that they have very good reasons for concealing who they are. Perhaps they are in danger or some such thing.''

Dominic gave another low laugh. There was something irritatingly sensual about it. ''And I said that you did not have an imagination,'' he murmured. ''I am gratified that you have such a sense of loyalty to the Wellbornes.'' She felt the force of those dark eyes full upon her. ''I wish that I had earned it.''

She was momentarily rendered speechless.

''Athena! What are you doing, girl? Don't just stop dead in the street! I was in the middle of a conversation!''

''Sorry, Auntie,'' Athena mumbled. She pushed the chair to catch up to Dominic and Lord Falk.

''The girl's gone as absent as you, Falk. Next thing you know she'll be spouting nonsense about my beautiful eyes. Attics to let, the both of you. I thank heaven every day I didn't marry you. Dealing with a gouty old fuss-bucket like you on a daily basis would have positively unhinged me.'' She gave her dusty cackle. ''I would be the one going to London, but to the Ladies' Prison for strangling you.''

''No doubt,'' he agreed cheerfully, ''for a more violent, bad-tempered creature was never born. Here, stop your infernal badgering. We are behind the Abbey and out of its freezing shadow, so let us sit in the sun for a moment.''

Athena pushed her aunt's chair into a sunny spot and stood behind it, chafing her cold hands. ''I know you are not a spy,'' she said at last in an undertone to Solage. ''You will laugh at me, I know, but I did have reasons for thinking ... thinking what I thought," she finished awkwardly.

"Indeed, I long to hear them," he replied with a twisted smile.

She dragged her eyes from his face. "In the book that you loaned me I found a list of names."

"Diantre!" he cut her off. "Little wonder—" He shook his head.

Her stomach gave an uncomfortable twist. He knew of the list then. It wasn't all some horrible, easily explained mistake.

"It is indeed little wonder you thought I was a spy." He looked away, his lips compressed for a long moment. "Athena, I cannot explain everything to you, much that I wish that I could." He did not seem to notice that he had used her first name. "You must allow me my secrets for the time being." He must have seen her hesitant expression because he laughed. "I see now that it is ridiculous that I should ask for your trust. I will not mention the incident in my apartments again, For such carelessness, I should be punished, and so I have been, by being unable to explain myself to someone such as you. You could have given me such valuable advice." His eyes went soft. "I wish that I had met you many years ago. Ah, but I was too stupid then. I would never have appreciated your wisdom."

She forced herself to frown. Surely this was merely said to flatter her ego. "I do not like you when you are being sarcastic Monsieur Solage, but I like you even less when you are being insincere." She cursed herself for being so naïve as to wish that he would banter with her as he had on the night of the assembly. That he would touch her like he did that night.

"Ah." Falk drew in a deep breath with every evidence of satisfaction. "This is just like the old days." He slapped his waistcoat and looked around. "Damn awful weather, insufferable Bath company, the country in crisis again with that Corsican running amok, and old Louisa as crotchety as ever."

Auntie Montie sniffed. "The company in Bath will be a good deal less insufferable once you are gone. I would ask you to convey my regards to the Castlereaghs when you are in town, but I am certain that you would only forget." She skewered him with a look from her narrowed eyes. "Fat, gouty, old men are very prone to senility I hear."

"I haven't forgotten the house party at Badminton," he replied with what could only be described as a leer.

Athena watched in amazement as Auntie Montie jumped and turned several shades of pink. She was distracted from this interesting transformation by Dominic's hand on her own. She felt the warmth of it through her glove. The hair along her arm rose up in a wave of . . . alarm? Was it alarm?

"Athena." His pronunciation of her name gave it a very foreign caress. "I know that I do not have the right to ask you to do anything." He continued to hold her hand and look directly into her eyes. He probably wanted to make sure that she was paying attention to what he was saying, but it was having the most opposite effect imaginable. She forced herself to drag her gaze away from his and focused on his mouth instead. "But I will ask anyway," he continued. "The Wellbornes. Do not listen to them too sincerely. Ah, but what am I saying?"

She had no idea what he was saying. Watching his mouth move had the strange effect of suddenly making her wonder what it would be like to kiss him.

"I cannot explain, my dear, but you must do as I say." The pressure of his hand on hers brought her thoughts back to the present.

"What?" she said sharply. "Sophia and Charles?" She extricated her hand from his. It suddenly felt cold again. "It always comes back to them doesn't it? I do not understand this vendetta of yours. I was foolish to come into your house, but you were happy to upbraid me for it until you found out my reasons. Then you are completely willing to admit your fault in the whole debacle and concede entirely that I was correct in assuming what I did. But you refuse to explain yourself!" She felt the exhilaration of righteous indignation buzz through her cold limbs. If she was angry with him, if she saw him for the insincere bounder that he was, perhaps she would not be so dangerously attracted to him.

"And then"—she hissed triumphantly—"you have the impertinence to tell me how to manage my friendships!" She drew back and set her hands on her hips. "Really, Monsieur Solage, your audacity is astounding!" She would very much have liked to have made a incensed exit after making this dramatic pronouncement, but Auntie Montie continued to be in deep conversation with Lord Falk. She did not look at Dominic, but she felt him staring at her in silence as she glared stonily toward the river.

"You do not recall the incident?" Falk asked in surprise. "Indeed, I think that you must be the one becoming forgetful in your old age, Louisa. When I am tucked away in cold, bleak London, I will while away my time by writing you a long account of the Badminton house party as I remember it." Athena did not mean to eavesdrop, but she could not miss Falk's completely audible announcement.

"Must you speak at the top of your lungs?" Auntie Montie snapped. "You are going deaf as well as dull-witted. And I will not countenance your writing me. Athena! Take me home immediately! And to think that I thought you might have changed in the last twenty years!'' She gave a little cry of alarm as Athena wheeled the chair around with more speed than skill.

''I will be back in two weeks, Louisa!'' Falk called out cheerfully after them as they barreled recklessly back toward the Pump Room. He chuckled to himself for a moment. ''She's a piece of work, ain't she, Solage?''

''Indeed she is,'' he replied quietly, still looking at the place where they had disappeared around the corner.

''Gets her back up if you so much as sneeze in her direction.'' He laughed again. ''I asked her to marry me back in ninety-five. She wouldn't look at me for ten years, wouldn't speak to me for twenty.'' He squinted up at the pale March sun. ''She can hold a grudge for a long time, that old baggage.'' He turned to Solage and grinned. ''But she can carry the torch for longer. I'd say she is well on her way toward being head-over-rheumatic heels for me again.'' He winked. ''I've still got it!''

Dominic looked at him for a moment as though he had just begun to listen to what he was saying. ''I never doubted that, sir,'' he replied solemnly.

''Damn but you're a dull dog! Push me back home. Did you see how she was looking at me? Blushed pink as a girl, she did!'' he crowed. ''The old iceberg was getting a bit weak at the stiff old knees!'' He slapped his own knees in glee. ''What's the matter with you, Solage? Don't tell me you were too distracted by that poker-faced niece to see my triumph!''

Dominic bridled, but restrained himself from replying. It would only give Falk more ammunition. ''I hope you are not trifling with Miss Louisa Montgomery's affections,'' he said, trying to sound teasing. There was nothing poker-faced about Athena. She was not so conventionally pretty as her sister to be sure, but there was a certain . . . radiance about her, especially when she laughed. Good God he was sounding ridiculous—even to himself.

Falk chuckled. "Are you going to call me out, Solage? I can see us now. You pushing my chair out to ten paces and then having to walk all the way back to your mark to shoot me. Heh! Heh! Ah those Miss Montgomerys! What about the other one? Now that you've nearly compromised her, you could give her an offer she wouldn't refuse. Daresay she'd be delighted. You'd be Castlereagh's nephew-in-law, you know. Wouldn't do your political career any harm."

"What are you talking about?" Dominic stared at him. The man was going soft in the head. He surreptitiously wheeled the chair out of the direct sunlight.

Falk rolled his eyes impatiently. "The pretty niece. The one you caught poking about my house. Let that news out and you could marry her in two shakes of the parson's forefinger!" He shook his finger at Solage with a comic expression of censure.

"I am afraid that you have misunderstood," he replied calmly. "The young lady that you just met was the niece that was in your house."

"That one!" Falk's watery gray eyes popped open. "The bluestocking? The one that has set Bath on its ear by playing chaperone?" He blinked several times. "She isn't nearly as plain as they say. Rather fine eyes in fact. Too starchy by half, though. Didn't think she had the spirit to go romping about some stranger's house without a by-your-leave. Castlereagh's oldest niece, eh? I thought she was being courted by that deWit scoundrel. Louisa never would have countenanced *that* match, you may be sure of that. Well, you'd better damn well hope that no one leaks out the story of her being in your bedroom. Either be forced to marry Castlereagh's Friday-faced niece or the elusive female Mr. deWit of the Jamaica Isles scheme!" He laughed long and hard. "The Committee would love that match, you may be sure!"

"I don't believe I intend to marry either of them," he replied as he began wheeling Falk's chair up the hill toward the house on Rivers Street. He pictured for a moment what it would be like to be married to Athena. She would shine as a literary hostess. With her intellect, she could discuss the weightiest subjects with the foremost experts on the most even of footings. But really it was not her intelligence he loved. There was something in that dry wit, something in her appreciation of the ridiculous.

His thoughts came to a grinding halt. Had he said loved? Well, of course he meant it only in the sense of general admiration. Admiration that stemmed from their mutual interest in literature. It was a natural appreciation that anyone would feel who came to know her well. She was nothing that she appeared to be. Well, no. She was everything she appeared to be and yet more. What was wrong with him? He gave himself an impatient shake. What was he thinking to wax poetic over a silly chit who couldn't bear to be in the same room with him?

Besides, Castlereagh would have his hide if he knew that he was courting his niece. He would think it the grossest imposition on his role as courier/advisor to Falk and the Committee. And Athena herself would likely look at the liaison as though he were only marrying her to get ahead in the political world. But what was he thinking!

"God's nightcap, Solage! There is no need to go so fast!" Falk shouted. "What do you think this is, a racing curricle? I daresay you think you feathered that turn rather nicely, you young whip. Next thing you be trying to drive through gates without taking the paint off the chair. I'm likely to lose an arm!"

"My apologies, Falk. I thought that you were in a hurry to get home," Dominic replied sheepishly.

"I shall have to get a little tiger to ride up behind the

chair. He can hold my reins and walk me up and down the street when you go calling on people!''

''I am going very slowly now, do you see? I hope I did not hurt your leg.''

''We can pick the wheels of the chair out in yellow, don't you think?'' Falk was warming to the subject. ''And we shall get you a driving coat with capes down to your heels! Tally ho!'' He brandished his cane wildly.

Dominic pushed the chair up to the front of the town house at a funeral pace while Falk whooped and pretended to whip up a team in front of him. ''I see now why Miss Louisa Montgomery ceased speaking to you,'' he said dryly.

Chapter Fourteen

Cass gesticulated impatiently from the doorway of the Pump Room as she saw them cross the courtyard. "Athena! Where have you been? I have been waiting for you a half hour. I thought perhaps that you had gone home without me."

"No, of course not. Auntie and I just wanted to get some air. I am so sorry that you have had to wait."

Cassiopeia's mouth tightened into a pout. "It would not have surprised me if you had left me. No one ever gives me the least thought. The only reason I exist is to be married off and become somebody's brood mare."

"Cass!" Athena gasped. "Don't say such a thing. You know it isn't true."

"'Course it is," Auntie Montie snapped. "It is the only reason any woman exists. Those of us who are lucky are born rich enough to live independently, but not so rich that we'll attract fortune hunters, and are born plain enough not to have our heads filled with stupid notions of romance," she continued savagely. "You're either a brood mare or a spinster, and I'll tell you what—I would much rather be the latter rather than be shackled to some damned old fool who doesn't give two shakes for you, keeps you eternally breeding, and has a mistress on the side."

Cass gave a start and began to cry. Athena stopped and attempted to hug her sister, but the Bath chair was on a slope and kept trying to roll back down the hill. "Here, darling, don't cry. Everyone is staring. You know Auntie doesn't mean what she said." She lowered her voice to a whisper. "She is very cross right now."

"I certainly am. And if I was your mother, I would box both of your ears for acting as though I were deaf."

"She is very cross," Athena repeated loudly with a wink to Cass, "because she just had to deal with the most impertinent old man. He was *terribly* old, so I would not be surprised if he were not a little insane."

"He is not old!" Auntie Montie objected. "Impertinent he may be, but he is not a day over eighty. Five," she tacked on belatedly "And he is sharp as a tack, that man. And a great statesman! Your mother should have taught you to respect your elders, you hussies. He is a great crony of your Uncle Castlereagh's, so if you ever want a Season in London, you would do well not to speak ill of that man."

"Old beau," Athena mouthed to her sister as she continued to push the chair up the hill. Cass's brows rose in surprised interest, her grievous neglect temporarily forgotten. The footman who usually pushed Auntie Montie's chair home from the Pump Room came flying down the hill to them.

"So sorry, miss, I waited at the Pump Room at the usual time, but you did not appear, so I thought you had gone home," he said, panting. He took the chair from Athena and began pushing it vigorously up the hill.

"It is fine, Andrew. We met up with some acquaintances and went for a walk behind the Abbey Church. Miss Cassiopeia and I were able to manage without you thus far, though I am happy you have arrived."

"Blunderhead!" Auntie Montie exclaimed, craning over her shoulder to glare at the footman. "You should have waited. And slow down. There is no need to shake all my bones apart, sirrah. And you, Athena, don't speak about me as though I were not here. I will be the one to berate my servants, missy."

"I never doubted that, ma'am," she replied serenely.

"Who was this beau?" Cass asked with interest, pulling Athena's arm so that they dropped behind their aunt, who continued to unleash her pent-up wrath on the hapless servant.

"Lord Falk," Athena reluctantly replied. "I don't believe you know him." She was not about to go into the details of how she herself knew the man.

Cass shrugged and showed no further interest. "Well, I think you might have told me that you were leaving," she said peevishly. "It was humiliating to be there unescorted. No one appears to care about my reputation in the least."

She took her sister's arm. "You know that is not true, Cass. I saw that you were walking with Sophia. I can't very well take care of both you and Auntie at the same time."

"I don't need to be taken care of," she countered irritably. "But I am beginning to feel like so much chattel."

"What are you talking about?"

"My whole purpose in coming here was to get married. Everyone wants to be rid of me. I can't help it if I was not born clever like you. Mama and Papa only want me to be married off so that they don't have to worry about their poor foolish disappointment of a daughter.'' Cass ignored her sister's sputtered protests and continued. ''Char—that is, someone was saying that I shall be sold off to the highest bidder without the least regard for my feelings in the matter.''

''But you know that isn't true. Mama and Papa would never have you marry where your feelings are not engaged. And,'' she reminded Cass pointedly, ''you were the one who begged to come here for a Season. They would have been happy to keep you at home for another year and then had a proper come-out in London next year.''

''By then I would have been an old maid,'' Cass replied, the illogic of her own argument lost on her. ''And now, now I have met the only man I could ever care about and Auntie has sent him packing!''

''What are you talking about?'' Athena felt her world spinning.

''I am in love with Charles Wellborne,'' she replied defiantly. ''But yesterday Auntie has said that he is no longer welcome at the house. She had the rudeness to call him a fortune hunter to his face!'' Her color rose in indignation.

''Do you really love him?'' Athena gasped.

Cass scowled ferociously. ''Of course I do. There is no need to look so disapproving. You are just as bad as Auntie. Sophia is the only one who understands.''

''No, no,'' Athena put in quickly, ''I do not disapprove in the least. Charles Wellborne is a—very worthy man.'' She felt a blush heat her cheeks. Should she tell Cass that Charles had already proposed to *her?* That might only be hurtful. ''I just hope that you will be prudent and . . . and make sure that this is a lasting attachment.''

"Prudent," Cass spoke the word with scorn. "You have never been in love, Athena, or you would not speak of prudence."

Athena was glad that they had reached the house, and she was not obliged to reply.

"I just hope that you will be prudent, Athena." Sophia smoothed the pale green muslin of her morning gown and then looked up with an expression of concerned sincerity.

"I don't know quite what you mean," she replied stiffly.

"Solage." Sophia spoke the word with a hiss. "I left the Pump Room yesterday and I just happened to see that you were promenading behind the Abbey Church with none other than Lord Falk and Monsieur Solage."

It occurred to Athena that in order to see her and Auntie Montie behind the Abbey Church, Sophia must have gone very much out of her way, but she only raised her brows questioningly.

"Don't tell me you have fallen under his charming spell, Athena!" Sophia asked in horror. "Solage is a danger to England itself!"

"Such fustian!" she exclaimed dismissively. "I was caught up in the moment, too, Sophia, but it is time for us to admit that there is nothing in the least bit mysterious about Monsieur Solage."

"Oh dear," her companion moaned dramatically. "He has seduced your reason with his silvered words."

An errant thought escaped into Athena's consciousness that she would rather enjoy more than her reason being seduced by Solage, but she forced herself to focus on what Sophia was saying.

"He is a dangerous man. Even if he were not a spy, which I am convinced he is. After all, those letters from his sister could be in code, you know. But besides his possible nefarious connections, he is not the kind of man a single woman in possession of a good reputation should associated with. Oh I know''—she waved her hand dismissively—''that he is accepted everywhere, but the fact remains that he could ruin both of our reputations in one fell swoop if he were to let out the story that we were in his chambers alone.''

''He would not do that,'' Athena replied quietly. She thought of Solage's warnings against the Wellbornes and suddenly felt irritated with both him and Sophia. Why was everyone of her acquaintances insisting that everyone else was dangerous and not to be trusted. Apparently all of Bath was populated with plotting evildoers. She grimaced. ''Solage was very gentlemanly about the incident, and we have agreed to forget the entire thing.''

''I am certain that he was,'' Sophia said meaningfully, ''but I would hate to see my dear friend's reputation ruined because she believed the word of a very insincere man. You know he is thought to be quite the dashing rake. Half the ladies in Bath are swooning over him, and I just don't wish for you to be heartbroken because of his gallantry. I would hate for any talk to be bandied about because you are seen too often with him. They are already calling him 'Athena's Conquest,' you know. I know that you were raised in a very sheltered atmosphere. You must trust that I know a good deal more about the ways of the world than you. Indeed, though you are very intelligent, and I don't doubt a good deal more educated than a woman should be, you are very naïve when it comes to the ways of society.''

It occurred to Athena in a flash of annoyance that her reputation would not have been endangered if it had not been for Sophia's plans to infiltrate Falk's house. But she simply pressed her friend's hand. ''I thank you. You are kind to warn me. And you are right. Solage is a very charming man, but I assure you, he does not have any effect on me. And I am certain that he thinks of me as nothing more than a plain old spinster with a very pretty sister. As with every man, he thinks to get to Cass by making up to me.'' She shrugged lightly and pressed down the fervent hope that that was not true.

Andrew the footman slipped into the room and coughed urgently. ''Excuse me, Miss Montgomery, but Monsieur Solage is here. Will you see him?''

Athena felt a wash of panic. Of all times for him to call! Her feelings for him were all a jumble. Yesterday she had quarreled with Solage over his interfering in her friendship with the Wellbornes and now she was quarreling with Sophia over her friendship with Solage. ''Show him up,'' she said with a great deal more self-possession than she felt.

''Really, Athena!'' Sophia exclaimed, ''I think that you should send that man packing. He is a good deal too dangerous to continue an acquaintance with.'' She would have continued, but Solage himself entered the room.

''Miss Montgomery.'' He bowed toward her. ''And, Miss Wellborne, as well. Indeed, my pleasure is doubled.'' There was a tightness about his mouth that belied his gallant statement. ''I know that your aunt dislikes visitors, but I hoped that I could prevail upon you to go walking with me. I do not know if you have seen the city from Beachen Cliff already, but this is a particularly clear and fine day.''

Athena opened her mouth to reply, but Sophia jumped in first. ''Miss Montgomery is engaged to me for the afternoon.''

''Perhaps we could both go with you, Monsieur Solage,'' she countered sweetly. There. That should spike both their guns. Let them hash out their differences once and for all. She felt a slight, wicked pleasure as both parties regarded her in horror.

Dominic recovered first. "Of course. I would be delighted."

"Indeed," Sophia agreed with a frosty smile.

"Grand. Then I will just run up to tell my aunt where we are going if you would be so good as to collect our coats, Sophia. We can be on our way immediately." She smiled brightly as she sailed from the room.

"I have always longed to see the view from Beachen Cliff. I cannot believe that I have been in Bath above a month and never had the opportunity to walk out here. I daresay it is because Cassiopeia is not overfond of walking, and of course, Auntie cannot manage it. But even so, I really should have come up here long ago."

Dominic knew Athena was prattling in order to fill the awkward silences, but there was something so charming about it that he did not step in to help her.

"What a very fine day it is today," she finished lamely.

"It is indeed," he agreed, finally relenting.

"The top at last," he exclaimed as they pulled up on the scenic overlook. "I do not think that they have anything like this in Scarborough, Miss Wellborne." Forget Athena, he chided himself. This was a prime opportunity to find out more about the mysterious Miss deWit.

"No, there is not," she replied.

"Is there in France?" Athena asked.

"Nothing so beautiful."

"Where are you from in France?"

"Rouen. Have you been there?"

"No. Unfortunately, I have been unable to travel the Continent."

"For obvious reasons," Sophia interjected pointedly.

"I must take you there someday," he replied mildly, smiling at Athena. He watched as she blushed in confusion.

"What a lovely view!" she exclaimed again, pressing her hands to her cheeks.

"I am happy that you thought to bring sketching material, Miss Montgomery. The light is very good, and I am sure that you have both been trained in sketching."

"Actually," Athena said ruefully, "I was never taught the arts of sketching and watercolors. I know that you must think that it is part of the requisite education of every young lady of quality in England, but I am afraid that my family was much more unconventional." She reluctantly took the charcoal pencil that he proffered and examined it with interest. "The emphasis was more on languages and philosophy than needlework, pianoforte, and watercolors."

He looked at her with interest. "How dare you speak as though you were ashamed." She stared at him for a moment, her gray eyes wide, then smiled with a little breathy laugh. He dragged his attention to Miss Wellborne. "But you must surely draw, Miss Wellborne."

"I am afraid I do not either, Monsieur Solage," she replied with an uncomfortable laugh. "How shocked you must be to find that the education of English ladies is not at all what you were told." Her smile was bright but stiff. "However I cannot excuse myself. I cannot claim to be educated by parents devoted to the Wollstonecraft principles. My father was more addicted to the faro tables than philosophy, and my mother had a hard enough time keeping food in our mouths. I'm afraid that Charles and I were left to scrabble very much for ourselves. There was little time for watercolors. But I am sure that you know all of this already." She leveled a penetrating glare at him, daring him to deny it.

"I am delighted," he said jovially. "How terrified I have been that I was in the presence of masters. I have always wanted to sketch, but have never had the opportunity either. Now we may all attempt to capture this picturesque landscape without the least regard to skill or training."

Athena smiled gratefully at him. "We will have a competition to see who has the most natural raw talent. I can assure you that mine will likely look like nothing but a few wavy lines. She cheerfully saw that everyone was supplied with paper and pencil and then sat down to sketch.

Dominic scratched away at the paper for a few moments but was soon distracted. He pretended idly to draw, but instead watched Athena over the top of his page. She sat on a rock with a look of intense concentration on her face, her head tilted slightly to the side as she contemplated the city below. She was all graceful curves, the arch of her long neck and slim wrists complementing the line of her back as she sat slightly turned from him, her gray pelisse making it appear that she was formed from the rock on which she sat.

His hand began to move without him even meaning for it to. He traced on the paper the tip of her nose and the curve of her chin as they peeped out from the edge of the new bonnet. He smiled to himself. It was a rather nice bonnet, even if he did resent its eclipsing her features. She would be lovely if she wished to be.

"Oh dear," she said irritably. "This looks like a spider with the pox." She held up a rather shaky representation of the city. "I declare myself the loser of the competition. I think I had better stop and take up a new hobby." Dominic's hand paused as she stood up and shook out her skirts. "How is yours going, Sophia?" She leaned over her friend's paper.

"Not very well I'm afraid," Sophia replied. "I have only managed the top of the Abbey Church."

"But it is very good. I can tell exactly what it is. I think that you have cheated, Sophia. We were all supposed to be amateurs." She walked over to where Dominic sat. "And you, Monsieur Solage? Will you shame me too?"

He quickly covered his portrait of her with his sleeve. "I am afraid that I have hardly done anything. I suppose I was too distracted by the beauty of the day."

She scrutinized preliminary scratches of the skyline for a moment. "It is very good. What a pity that you did not continue. I am afraid that I must disqualify you for incomplete workmanship." She laughed brightly. "Sophia is our winner. Now, Sophia, as the winner you may request anything you wish."

Sophia regarded them both with an expression of bitterness. "I wish," she said coldly, "to be driven home."

Chapter Fifteen

"We shall all be murdered in our beds," Lady Battford said with a certain doleful satisfaction.

"Of course we shall." Her husband carefully dusted the snuff from his sleeve. "It is all over now. With Napoleon arrived in Paris with that army of zealots he amassed, it won't be more than a week before we are part of the Empire." He sighed dramatically. "Not even Wellington will be able to do a thing."

Athena frowned and looked about the salon. Mrs. Reading-Thrandle was hosting what was supposed to have been a musicale, but no one seemed able to do anything but discuss the new development in France. "Well, I am certain that there is no reason to panic just yet," she said calmly.

Her hostess clutched Athena's arm. "Paris fallen! Have you heard anything from your uncle? Does he say that we should flee? Perhaps Scotland would be safe. I can't think of why anyone would want to invade somewhere so damp.'' Her fingers relaxed as she mused. ''Mr. Reading-Thrandle has a house in Aberdeen for the grouse season. I have never been there myself, as I could never abide grouse either dead or alive. I think it was because I was once very ill from a grouse pie as a child.''

''Mmmm,'' Athena inserted, with feigned interest.

''Though perhaps Ireland would be safer. I fancy the French wouldn't care to invade Dublin!'' Her chins quivered and her clutch tightened.

''Because it . . . ?''

Mrs. Reading-Thrandle's pale brows arched meaningfully. ''Because it is so terribly unfashionable,'' she whispered.

''Ah.''

''And you know how important fashion is to the French.'' She gave a sage nod.

Athena attempted to disengage her arm from her hostess's bruising grasp. ''Well,'' she said with a smile, ''I have heard nothing from my uncle, but I feel certain that the government is doing everything that is right in this crisis.''

''Of course we will get the French fashion plates so much sooner . . .'' Mrs. Reading-Thrandle continued to herself. ''In fact''—she brightened—''not only that, but once we are French ourselves, we will be ever so much more fashionable without even having to try!''

Athena took a glass of negus from a tray and glided away, leaving the woman to muse in private. Poor Anna Battford stood at the pianoforte looking nervously ready to begin her concert. However, there was no lull in the hubbub of conversation in the room, and the Reading-Thrandles did not appear inclined to announce the beginning of the entertainment. Athena took a sip of her drink and regarded the room across the rim of the glass. It was full of all the same people who went to every assembly.

The Wellbornes, however, were conspicuously absent. Since their bedridden grandmother was not able to introduce them into polite society, they were generally present at only the public gatherings.

She saw Cass sitting in a window seat with Celia Beetling. The two were surrounded by a clutch of admirers. Well at least she appeared to have gotten over her attachment to Charles Wellborne.

"We'd damn well better hang that Frenchman who's been hanging about town," she heard someone saying behind her.

"I don't trust any Frenchie. I'd lay a pony he's a spy."

"I said so from the first. He might be in cozy with Falk, but everyone knows the old man's nearly senile. We'll hang him tonight, Tanders, and then apologize later if it turns out that we were wrong."

She felt her knees sag and nearly dropped her glass. They couldn't possibly be serious. But even so, the populace was bound to turn against Solage very soon.

"A bit drastic, eh? What say we just box him up a bit or throw him in the Avon? That would get the message across."

She revolved slightly to see who was speaking, but her view was blocked by a potted plant. There were young bucks in town who would like nothing better than to stir up trouble in the name of patriotism. She moved forward slightly to try to get a look at them, but her attention was arrested by a woman's voice.

"I certainly hope that Monsieur Solage has had the sense to leave town. He won't be welcome here for long."

"Indeed," said her partner. "He was quite the fashion for a while, when Boney was in Elba, but now things are entirely different."

He must be warned. With Falk in London, Dominic had no one to vouch for him. Perhaps it would be better if he were to go up to London himself, where the society was less prone to panic and prejudice.

Suddenly every conversation in the room stammered to a halt. Athena turned expectantly to Miss Battford at the front of the room. The girl was staring in horror at the doorway, along with everyone else in the salon. Dominic Solage stood in the doorway, coolly surveying the crowd of faces turned upon him. Out of the silence, Mrs. Reading-Thrandle began a high, incomprehensible monologue and bore down upon him.

"Oh dear . . . Very unfortunate . . . I don't know how . . ."

Athena was at his elbow in a moment. "Monsieur Solage. How nice that you have arrived." She smiled up at him and raised her voice a notch. "My uncle Robert Castlereagh had just written to me to ask how you fared."

"Castlereagh?" A strange expression leapt into his eyes.

"Yes"—she shot him a meaningful look as she tucked her hand into his elbow and pulled him into the room— "and have you heard from Falk?"

"Yes, he is very well. He hopes to return to Bath soon."

The crowd parted like the Red Sea as they moved through the room. Mrs. Reading-Thrandle trailed after them, still sputtering.

"Miss Battford, I hope that we will hear your singing. I hear that you are extremely talented." Athena smiled serenely at the girl.

"Yes, Mrs. Reading-Thrandle, mightn't I start? I get so nervous just waiting," she said pleadingly.

"Well, my dear—that is—I am not certain that—Monsieur Solage, I must insist that—oh dear—I must—"

"Madam, were you waiting for my arrival to start the musicale?" Dominic turned to her and bowed gracefully. "How very thoughtful! But I should not be surprised. It is just the kind of thing that you would do, Mrs. Reading-

Thrandle.'' He smiled at her with a grateful look that Athena knew would have made her agree to anything if it had been turned upon herself.

The woman herself gave a faint whimper and then nodded her turbaned head toward Miss Battford. ''Yes, I suppose you'd better start. Oh dear. Where is my husband?'' She pushed distractedly through the crowd and disappeared.

Miss Battford stared at them curiously for a moment and then went to the pianoforte. Mr. Reading-Thrandle had been bestirred and stood up to announce with very little enthusiasm the titles of Miss Battford's selections. He mispronounced the name of every composer as well as Miss Battford's own name and was audibly corrected in a nervous hiss from his wife.

Athena was silently grateful for Reading-Thrandle's bungling. The attention of the other guests was now occupied in tittering at the little drama played out between their host and hostess. Dominic led her to a seat at the back of the room.

''Thank you,'' he said softly, pressing her hand as he let it go.

''Of course.'' She didn't know what to say. It had been terribly wrong to use Uncle Robert's name to extricate him from the mess. Of course her uncle didn't know Solage, but his name would lend him protection. It had been very foolish, but she simply had not been able to think of anything better at the time. He sat with one hand outstretched on his bent knee. His hands were long and slim. There was something very masculine about the squareness of his fingertips and the strong ridges where his veins stood out faintly blue against his skin. She forced herself to look away.

''It is strange that the one I thought trusted me the

least should trust me so much as to publicly declare my innocence.'' He regarded her without blinking.

She frowned. ''You make it sound so poetic. I only did it because . . . well, anyone would have. How stupid people can be!'' She felt a blush rise up her neck and turned to look at the floor with a sudden intent interest. ''I should know.''

''You were absolved long ago, Miss Montgomery,'' he said softly. ''Now it is I who am indebted to you.'' There was something painfully sensuous in his slow smile. ''I prefer it to be that way.''

She covered the flutter of confusion she felt by clasping her hands tightly in front of her and concentrating on Miss Battford's performance.

''You have a very nice frown, Miss Montgomery.''

''I don't know what you mean.'' She realized that she was indeed frowning and instantly shot him a brilliant false smile.

''You have an even more beautiful smile, but I think that I prefer the frown.'' He leaned over to peer into her averted face. ''The frown means that you are thinking, and I like it that you think.''

''What I am thinking now''—she tilted her chin up and regarded him steadily—''is that I would like you a good deal more if you were less charming and more sincere.''

He laughed. ''It always comes back to that, does it not? *Enfin*, I will try not to be charming and will only be charmed.'' He took her hand and pressed it. ''Miss Battford has paused. I must talk to our hostess and some of the other guests or people will begin to talk about us.'' She tried to remove her hand from his, but her arm did not respond.

He looked at her with a serious expression. ''You are a very intelligent woman, my warrior goddess, but I believe that sometimes you would do better to think with your heart rather than your head.''

She jerked her fingers back and clutched them to her. He could see straight through her. He knew she had fallen in love with him despite her high-minded primness and public espousal of spinsterhood.

''Spare me your platitudes, Solage,'' she snapped when he was almost out of hearing. She could hear his quiet laughter in reply.

''What did you go and do that for?'' Cass demanded as she dropped into the chair Dominic had recently vacated.

''What?'' Athena looked at her sister with a vague expression of confusion.

''Announce to the world that Uncle Robert knows him!''

She sighed and rubbed her hand across her aching forehead. ''I don't know. I really don't. I shouldn't have, I know. I suppose I thought that it would give him the necessary cachet to keep people from hanging him.''

Cass looked surprised. ''Well, I hardly think that they would have done that. Mrs. Reading-Thrandle would never have allowed it in her drawing room, in any case. But really, Athena, with Napoleon in Paris, Solage should not be surprised if he is shunned by polite society. After all, we know virtually nothing about him.'' She opened her gray eyes wider. ''I have always thought that there was something sinister about him.''

''What? Are you daft? A week ago you were flinging yourself at him!''

Her sister looked offended. ''Indeed I was not. At least,'' she amended, ''not very much. In any case, I am very much more wise to his character now.''

''I don't see how you can be. It is much more likely that you have been listening to the vindictive nonsense of Charles Wellborne.''

Cass's face turned an angry red. "Don't you dare say anything about Charles! You are only jealous! You are spiteful because you were sweet on him until he saw you for the nasty cat that you are." Her eyes narrowed. "You should be careful what you say, Athena." She stood up with a flounce. "You never know what may happen."

"If you mean that he will spread ridiculous rumors about me as well, I am hardly worried."

Her sister sniffed. "I am tired and I am going home. I will have a footman call a sedan chair, so there is no need for you to bestir yourself to come with me. After all," she shot back over her shoulder, "no one considers you a fit chaperone anyway."

Dominic bowed over his hostess's limp hand and moved over to sit next to the Battfords. Poor Mrs. Reading-Thrandle had been entirely unable to respond to his rather gratuitous praise of her party, her home, and her looks of good health.

"I see that your daughter is going to continue her concert. She is very talented, Miss Battford." It would be interesting to see if the rest of the audience were as tongue-tied. He repressed a wave of irritation that washed over him. Curse Bath society! Gossips, all of them. But it was his own fault, too; he should have insisted on accompanying Falk to London.

"Indeed she is," Lady Battford replied curtly. She eyed him suspiciously for a moment. "How are you, Monsieur Solage?"

"I am well. Though I must confess, I am a little anxious about my sister. She lives in Paris with her husband and two daughters. As a loyal subject to the king, she must be very anxious now that Napoleon has arrived in the city."

Lady Battford's expression melted into sudden sympathy "Oh dear, she must be terrified! Can they not flee Paris? They will be murdered in their beds!"

"Most certainly," Lord Battford agreed.

Dominic wished for a moment that he had not brought up the subject of Adèle. After all, why should he have to justify himself to these gossipmongers? He thought of how Athena had stepped to his side and neatly forced everyone in the room to treat him civilly. For a moment he had feared she knew of his connection to her uncle, but it appeared she had merely used his name to impress the crowd. "Actually"—he lowered his voice under the beginning bars of Miss Battford's ballad—"my sister wrote that there is a good deal of unrest. The support for Napoleon is not as strong as you might think. She suspects that this coup will not be successful."

Miss Battford began singing at that moment, but her parents' brows both rose in interest. Dominic smiled slightly. Of course now they were dying to press him for more information. He leaned back in his chair and listened to the music. The smile faded. He hoped Adèle was right. Her letters had been very confident, but of course she knew that he would be on the first ship back to France if she said that things were getting out of hand. He wished now that he had forced her and her family to come with him to England. But her husband was a stubborn old goat if there ever was one and refused to abandon Paris. He somehow thought that if he were not there to direct things, the entire city would fall into a panic.

It sounds very much like yourself, he could almost hear Athena's voice saying sharply. Well, perhaps it did. He turned his head slightly and looked for her. She was sitting by herself with an absent expression on her face. He wished that she would frown. That frown showed her spirit. It showed that she was fighting against that side of her nature that she did not want to admit existed. Right now she only looked sad.

"Marvelously talented. You are certainly blessed." He sprang to his feet as soon as the music had stopped and murmured his praises to the Battfords. He was heading for Athena's chair before they could detain him with further questions about the state of affairs in France.

"Will you accompany me for a small walk on the balcony? I have requested that your cloak be brought, so you do not have to worry about catching the cold."

Her gray eyes flew to his in surprise. "Oh. Well. I don't seem to have a choice, do I?"

"Not really." He took her hand to help her rise and then put her cloak around her shoulders. "Let us slip out very quickly before the next singer begins." He pulled her toward the long doors that led out to the balcony. "There," he said as the oppressive heat of the drawing room was closed in behind them, "I have you to myself."

"It is much more pleasant out here." She drew a quick breath. "I think I was stifling in there." She walked to the stone balustrade and leaned out into the night. "We have already conversed this evening. Why did you need me to yourself?" She did not turn to face him.

"Athena"—with one step he was standing close behind her—"I enjoy to make you angry sometimes, but I never intend to make you sad. What have I done to make you look so unhappy?"

"Good heavens, but you are arrogant." Her voice in the darkness was tired. "If I seem out of sorts it has nothing to do with you, however shocking you may find that prospect."

He moved to lean on the balcony railing beside her, carefully keeping his elbow from touching hers. What a difficult woman. She rejected all of the polished manners and elaborate praise that he had been trained to present.

He had always relied on his charm to get him anything that he wanted and now it seemed that it was a liability. "Then what is making you unhappy?" he asked simply.

She sighed and looked up at the sky for a moment before she answered. "I don't think I can really talk about it," she said at last. "It is a family matter." She walked a few steps away from the light of the French doors. "It is very kind of you to be concerned though. Believe me when I say that I would tell you if I could." There was a long pause between them. "It is a very clear night," she said at last.

He followed her into the darkened corner. Her pale blue dress looked white in the darkness and made her seem slightly ethereal in the shadows. Did she have any idea what she was doing? Was this the prim Miss Montgomery's attempt at seduction? "Very clear," he replied. Surely she felt the pull between them, too. He would do nothing until he was sure. A mistake would destroy the small trust that was built up between them.

"The moon will be new in a day or two," she said softly, her face still up to the sky.

There was a sliver of it left in the darkness like a scratch on the sparkling surface of the sky. "Yes," he said hoarsely. He wanted to take her in his arms, but he shoved his fists into his pockets instead. Or rather, he tried. He found that his evening knee breeches did not sport pockets, so he crossed his arms awkwardly across his chest instead.

"This is not the best view, I'm afraid." She turned around with her back to the railing and leaned backward over it. "You can't see the eastern horizon at all. Can you imagine the view from Beachen Cliff tonight?"

Dominic regarded the slim paleness of her form as she arched backward over the balustrade. "Spectacular." He dragged his eyes away from the curve of her exposed neck and watched the flambeaux of the linkboys bob up the streets. There was something warm and bright about those twinkling earthbound fireflies. The stars above them were much colder in their pinprick brightness. The pianoforte inside sounded tinny and far away. "Are you cold?"

"Not in the least," she replied without moving. "It is much too hot inside." She seemed almost unaware that he was with her. "Look"—she pointed upward—"there is Cassiopeia."

"Where?"

She stepped beside him, pressing one hand to his folded arms and pointing to the stars with the other. Her cheek was very close below his own. "There. Do you see the North Star? It is there." Her white finger moved slightly in front of them. "Those stars shaped like a W."

He considered pretending not to see what she meant, just to keep her beside him. "I see," he said instead.

"It is supposed to be her crown." He could feel her breasts brush against his sleeve as she breathed. Her hand dropped, but she did not move away. "I was always envious of Cass for having a constellation. It somehow seemed fitting that she should be among the stars, while I am most prosaically here on earth."

"I am very glad that you are here on earth," he said softly. "I would never wish you among the stars."

She turned to him and his arms went around her of their own volition. "I don't believe I want to be anywhere else right now," she said softly. Then she rose onto her toes and kissed him.

For an instant he was so shocked that he couldn't respond. This wasn't the practical, cool Miss Montgomery he had come to know. She dropped down to her flat feet, evidently thinking that all there was to a kiss was a brief pressing together of lips. "Pardon me! I'm not sure why I—"

He cut off her apology with a second kiss. This one he was ready for. He felt her shocked paralysis melt quickly into a passionate response. Her body sagged slightly for a long moment, and then she gave him a sharp push.

"Stop it."

"Why?" Her honey-colored hair smelled faintly of soap and warmth. He inhaled deeply.

"I don't like this. I am falling apart."

"What is wrong with falling apart? It can be very pleasant."

She jerked herself out of his arms and pulled the edges of her evening cloak tighter around her. "No."

"Very well." He shrugged as though he did not care. "We will not attempt it again."

"Oh." She frowned in the way he liked. "Well. Thank you. It isn't—it isn't as though I didn't like it. It is just that—"

"I understand entirely," he said soothingly. "These things do not always work out."

"Oh no, it isn't that! It was—it was very—" She stopped herself and pulled awkwardly at her cloak. She cleared her throat. "Thank you very much. It was very pleasant."

He thought for a moment that she was going to hold out her hand and offer to shake his own. He covered his smile by rubbing his chin thoughtfully. "Yes, very nice," he said gravely. "Perhaps we should rejoin the party?"

She started. "I suppose we should. But I would really rather just go home." She looked miserably down at the streets of the city.

"I will tell the Reading-Thrandles that you were feeling . . ." He paused and savagely repressed another smile. "That you were feeling as though you were falling apart. And that you had to go home suddenly."

She narrowed her eyes at him, well aware that he was teasing her. "Precisely. Tell them that your embraces entirely undid me."

He laughed. "Your reputation is safe. After having found you in my bedchamber, I can hardly advertise to the gossips the mere fact that you were experimenting with kissing on the balcony. Very dull indeed."

"Yes, I was experimenting," she said faintly with a shaky laugh. "But you?"

He raised his brows and looked at her questioningly.

"That is, I know that you were only humoring me. There is no need for you to—that is, you need not fear that I took any of that the wrong way. I was only wondering how you were going home." Her face took on an expression of urgency. "Because I heard only just before you arrived that there were people who were planning to hang you, or at the very least injure you."

His mouth tightened. "Oh, I doubt that," he said lightly. "But it is very kind of you to warn me."

She turned again to look out on to the streets. "Well, of course." He saw the pale shoulders of her cloak rise and fall in a shrug. She turned to him. "So you will not walk home? You will be sure to take a chair? And ask it to wait until you are in the house before it drives on. Do you trust Falk's servants?"

He stopped her with a finger to her lips. "Enough, little goddess." She started to stammer her apologies, but he interrupted. "I will go inside and have someone order up a sedan chair to take you home. Wait a moment after me, my dear prudent Athena, before you come back to the salon." He gave her a wicked smile. "Or people will surmise that we have been doing . . . what we have been doing." He swiftly bent to kiss her behind her ear, enjoying her start of surprise. "Thank you for choosing me to be the subject of your ... experiment,'' he whispered against her skin.

He strode serenely back into the salon, well aware that he had infuriated her. Well, that was better than some blushing, stuttering apologies and several weeks of avoiding him. He rubbed his lips with his forefinger and thought of how it felt when she had responded so instantly to his embrace. Castlereagh. He reminded himself brutally. *One word of you seducing his niece on the Reading-Thrandles' balcony and you are off the committee and out of politics forever.* But who was seducing who?

Chapter Sixteen

Athena lay in bed and tried to recapture the very pleasant dream she had been having. It was no use. It was gone. Dreams were one thing, but had she really kissed Solage last night on the balcony? Had she really flung herself at him?

Of course he was polite to brush it off so easily when he easily could have tortured her with teasing or worse. She pulled the sheets tightly up to her chin. He could have ruined her reputation entirely. Cass was right. She was not a fit chaperone in the least. She slipped out of bed and pulled on her robe. Cass had been very upset last night. Perhaps she should have apologized to her when she got home last night, but her thoughts had been so much in a whirl that she honestly hadn't given her sister a thought.

She padded across the hall to her sister's room. After all, maybe she was just being churlish about Charles. It did seem fickle of him to have changed his affections so

quickly, but if he was genuinely in love with Cass . . .
She knocked softly at the door.

"Cass? I know it's early, but . . . Cass?" The room
was empty. "Cass," she sang out cheerfully as she peeked
into the dressing room. There was something wrong. The
bed was made and there were no wrinkles in the pink
coverlet. Nestled amongst the pillows was a sealed letter.
"Oh, Cass! You didn't!" She flew to the bed and broke
the seal on the note. She scanned it quickly and then let
out an inarticulate noise of frustration.

"Stupid!" She raced back into her own room and began
dragging on her clothes. She could only tie two of the
three tapes in the back of her green-and-white striped
gown, but it was the closest thing at hand and she didn't
have time to look for another. "Who cares. I'll keep my
coat on." She pulled on her pelisse, fighting to find the
second sleeve. "I'll kill you, Cass. I swear I will!" She
scuffed into a pair of lavender slippers that clashed violently with the gown. "No matter." She gave them a
scornful glance and darted to her writing desk. "Oh,
Auntie, Auntie, please don't be too cross today," she
muttered as she scrawled a few lies and sanded the paper.

"Andrew, please see that my aunt gets this when she
rises." She attempted an airy smile and thrust the note
into the hand of a footman on her way down the stairs.
Without looking back she could tell that he was still
standing on the steps where she had left him. "I'm going
out; I'll be back in a while!" She waved her hand, knowing that it only made her look more insane, and bounded
out the door.

"I will kill her. I will kill her," she chanted to herself
as she panted down Brook Street. "Then Mama will kill
me." She paused for a moment at the road off the circus
that led toward Rivers Street. What was she going to say?
She settled her bonnet straighter upon her head and wiped

the sweat from her forehead. But there was no one else. No one else she trusted.

What a strange thought, considering that not but a week ago she was breaking into that very house with the firm delusion that he was a spy. She closed her eyes to block out the memory. Before she had come to Bath she had thought she was a sensible, calm woman, not in the least bit prone to fancy, Gothic imaginings, or love. The specter of last night on the balcony elbowed into her mind, but she shoved it back. "Cass," she reminded herself tensely.

The ancient butler answered her knock, looking as pressed and professional as usual, despite the fact that it was only six in the morning. "I must see Monsieur Solage," she blurted out, realizing in an instant that she had not made up any excuse for her presence.

"What are you selling?"

She had forgotten he was nearly deaf. "Monsieur Solage!" she repeated clearly.

"Your hair is Spanish? What are you talking about, young lady? I am going to call the watch."

Desperate, she darted up the steps and tried to slip past him. He grabbed her by one wrist and the collar of her pelisse.

"What are you doing? Get out of here! This is a private residence!"

"Dominic!" she shouted up the stairs

"Mrs. Collins! Call the watch!"

"Dominic!" The butler was unexpectedly strong and had pushed her back onto the steps. He was attempting to shut the door on her arm when Dominic appeared at the head of the stairs.

"Ah. The lovely Miss Montgomery." He smiled pleasantly. "It is very early for wrestling with the butler, don't you think?"

"I must talk to you! It is most urgent!"

"This Spanish maniac is trying to sell you her hair!"

"I must say"—Dominic brushed the cuffs of his dressing gown in an infuriating gesture of boredom—"I do not understand English customs at all."

"Dominic!" She would kill him. First Cass, then him. He must have heard the desperation in her voice this time, because he came down the stairs and gently removed her from the butler's grasp. "What has happened?" He drew her into the library and shut the door.

"Cass has run off with Charles Wellborne!" She flapped the letter in his face. "They left sometime in the middle of the night. She says that Sophia has gone with them to act as chaperone until they get to Gretna Green."

Dominic's brows drew together. She saw that his gaze had dropped to her bosom and looked down to find that she had buttoned her pelisse one off so that it gaped and puckered all the way down. "It is a long way to Gretna Green," he said, almost to himself. "It would take them several days with even the fastest horses." He approached her and began absently rebuttoning her pelisse as if the disorder subconsciously bothered him. "Are you certain that is where they have gone?"

"It is what she said." Her voice came out a strangled pant. Somehow, all at once, she didn't give a damn about Cass and her troubles.

"And Miss Wellborne went with them," he mused, rubbing his thumb across the button closest to her chin. "And she was such a good friend to you."

Athena jerked away. "Yes, you may gloat all you wish. You told me all along that I should be wary of them." She folded her arms and regarded him balefully. "Everyone said all along that I was not a proper chaperone and that I could not control Cass, and now they have been proven right."

"You are becoming distracted from our purpose," he

said. She looked at him blankly, and he continued. "They have several hours' start, it is true, but there is every possibility that we will catch them before any lasting damage is done."

She exhaled. He had said "we." He meant to help her. "What first?" she asked, feeling strangely helpless.

"Wellborne did not own a carriage, so he must have hired one. I will send servants around to ask where he rented one. We may then begin to divine where they went."

"You don't think it was Gretna after all?" she asked in surprise.

He shrugged in that all-encompassing manner he had. "I do not know. You will wait here while I change, please. Perhaps you would like some tea? You should eat something too, as this may be a long day."

Things seemed to be moving very quickly. She felt a strange relief at being able to surrender some of her worry to him. "It would be best if none of the staff knew I was here," she said primly.

He threw back his head and gave a ringing laugh. "After you nearly engaged in fisticuffs with the butler while shouting the house down, I suspect that there is no one who does not know that you are here. I will have Mrs. Collins send you up something."

She stood still in the middle of the room for a long moment after he had left. How could Cass have been so foolish? It was not as though anyone would have forbidden her marriage to Charles if she had truly wanted it. Their family was well-enough off that Cass had the luxury of being able to marry whomever she pleased. She dropped into a chair beside the empty fireplace. She tried to picture her parents meeting the Wellbornes.

It was likely the Wellbornes who would be disappointed. The Montgomery household was anything but

fashionable. One was very likely to walk into the Montgomerys' to find her father and mother with their heads
together over a manuscript while the water for tea boiled
dry on the hob and the toast caught fire.

She looked up with a start as Mrs. Collins came in with
a tea tray, followed by a maid with a coal scuttle. "Can
I get you anything else, miss?" the housekeeper asked,
eyeing Athena with patent disapproval.

She shook her head. Dear heavens, her parents would
be upset when they heard the news of Cass's elopement.
Unconventional they might be, but scandal had never
touched the Montgomery family. She pressed her hands
to her temples and sighed.

"You are despairing already." Dominic had slipped
into the room without her hearing.

"No, I am only worried. Really, Monsieur Solage."
She stood up and smiled faintly. "I cannot thank you
enough for helping me. I am afraid that I was in a bit of
a panic, and you were the first person I thought to go
to."

He looked at her for a moment and then bowed slightly.
"That is a high honor indeed."

She felt a blush rise up in her cheeks, so she cleared
her throat and clasped her hands together in a businesslike
manner. "I am ready. What shall we do?" As if in answer
to her question, there was a scratch at the door and a
young boy appeared.

"What did you find out?"

"A swell like wot you said hired a closed rattler for a
golden boy a mile at the Headless Nun at eleven last
night. 'E tried to 'aggle it down but that was the cheapest
place in town and they wouldn't have none o' that. 'E
coughed up the rhino in the end, but 'e's a right nipfarthing
'e is."

Dominic looked at her with a blank expression. "What did he say?"

Athena addressed the boy urgently. "Did the innkeeper know where he was going in the carriage?"

" 'E drove into town." Athena's heart fell. That was no help. He drove into town to get Cass; the question was where did he go after that?

"Groom at the Nun said 'e asked 'ow long it took to get to Poole."

"Poole?" Dominic interrupted sharply.

"Not Gretna Green," Athena murmured. She turned to him. "I don't understand. She said herself that they were going to Gretna."

Dominic flipped a coin to the boy and put on his hat. "We will have to ask them." He smiled grimly and held open the door for her.

She looked at the closed carriage drawn up at the door with doubt. "Wouldn't a chaise be faster?"

He handed her in with an elaborate bow. "I would not dream of compromising your reputation by driving you across the country in an open carriage."

"Pooh. It is Cass's reputation we are worried about, not mine." The more she tried not to think about last night, the more vividly the memories washed over her. She glanced at him and saw by the slight twist of his mouth that he, too, was thinking of the kiss that they had shared.

"Yes," he said gravely, though there was a mocking twinkle in his dark eyes, "we need not worry about your reputation, after the"—he pretended to grope for a word—"disappointing results of last night's experiment."

She forced herself to scowl at him. "May I remind you that we are in a hurry?"

He stepped easily into the carriage and rapped sharply

on the roof to let the driver know to drive on. With a businesslike gesture, he checked his pocket watch. "*Voyons*. It is only six. They have only a two-hour start on us."

"Two hours? But Cass's note was dated at midnight!" She pushed the thoughts of last night on the balcony out of her mind. Later. She would savor them later—once Cass was safe. If only she were. "They could be anywhere by now!"

Dominic was watching the city spin past the window. "I suspect that they left closer to three or four. When was a woman ever ready to leave for a long journey on time? First she must be only half ready when he arrives, and then she must go through her baggage again to check to see if she really did pack something. That something must be at the bottom of the trunk and so necessitate unpacking the trunk entirely. Then once they are out of the house and in the carriage, she must realize that she has forgotten something else entirely and cannot leave without it."

"You are the most horrid, generalizing, stupid, misogynistic, creature I have ever had the misfortune to meet."

His brows rose slightly. "But for your sister, I am correct, no?" he asked cheerfully.

"It hardly matters," she snapped, hoping he was right, but at the same time wishing that he was not, so that she could skewer him with some stinging retort. "How do you propose to make up the time?"

"The horses are very fast," he replied with equanimity. "Lord Falk keeps a very good stable because he goes to London so often. I doubt that Mr. Wellborne, since he was unwilling to pay the price for the hire of a very cheap carriage, was willing to spend the money for good horses. Furthermore, he only has a pair, while we have four animals."

She nodded, unsure if even that would make up for a start of several hours.

"And," he continued, "he will only continue to go slower, because the job horses he will be able to get along the way will likely be very inferior."

Athena stared out the window, willing the horses to go faster. "But surely we will be slowed for the same reason," she countered. The horses were indeed well paced. They burst from the city streets and into the country without slackening their pace. She felt better once they were in the open air. Two hours though. At the very least they were two hours behind.

"We may be somewhat slowed by job horses," he conceded, steepling his long fingers together. "But I have brought along enough money to ensure that we are able to hire the best of what is available."

"Money!" She hadn't even thought about it. "Monsieur Solage, I swear I will pay you back. I left the house this morning in such a tizzy that I am lucky I remembered my head."

"Think nothing of it." He shrugged. "I am happy to be of service to you."

"I will keep track of everything you spend. I can never repay you for your help to me, but I will certainly repay the money." She thought for a moment. "I believe you must rue the day very much when you met the Montgomery sisters, Monsieur Solage. We have been nothing but trouble for you."

She had said it lightly, but he turned his eyes to her with a strange and serious expression. "Yes, Miss Montgomery," he said slowly, his eyes slightly narrowed as though a thought had just occurred to him. "You have been very troubling to me."

Chapter Seventeen

"Would your wife like some tea?"

He saw Athena's head jerk up. Her gray eyes were wide open and her mouth pressed shut as she waited to hear what he would say to the innkeeper.

"Would you like tea, my dear?" he asked solicitously. He smiled in satisfaction when she frowned. "I do not think that we have the time. I can see that your excellent hostlers have already changed the team." He pressed a coin into the innkeeper's palm. "We are trying to meet up with our friends. There was a tall, fair man, a young woman who is also fair, and a second young lady who is about so tall and has the hair of a light brown."

"A very pretty girl?" the innkeeper asked.

"Very pretty indeed,"

"Wearing a blue cloak?"

Dominic hesitated, but Athena exclaimed quickly. "Yes, yes she would be. That is, she is," she stammered.

"Did they change horses here? Did they continue on the Poole road?"

The innkeeper looked at her with some interest. "Yes, they did change horses here. They took a breakfast here, too. Quarreled something awful over it, because your young miss in the blue cloak wanted a private parlor and the tall, fair gentleman said that they would not have one."

"When were they here?" she demanded.

Dominic sighed and pressed another coin in the man's slightly outstretched hand. If she wouldn't seem so eager, they could probably get the information out of the man for free. This way only served to get his attention. But then if Adèle were in this kind of trouble . . . He put his arm around Athena's waist and pressed her hand to his lips. "My dear," he said kindly, "it is only a race. There is no need to be too caught up in it."

She looked up at him in shock, and he felt her begin to pull away and then still. "Of course." She gave a high, false laugh. "How silly of me. I do tend to get caught up in these things." She made a little gesture of dismissal that dislodged herself from his embrace. "But only if you had not bet so very much money on it, you naughty man!" She shook her finger at him playfully.

"A race eh?" The innkeeper rubbed his chin thoughtfully. "Not much competition, I should say. If the bloke were willing to shell out for cattle, he might have got the run on you, but he's a cheesenip, he is. Not only didn't want the private parlor, wouldn't let the ladies have more than porridge for breakfast and then got all pokered up about the hire of the horses." He laughed gruffly. "Now breakfast or not won't matter in your race, but calling me a cheat surely will. I gave him the slowest horses of the bunch. I'll not be accused of charging too high for my job animals. I charge same as other fellows around here."

"We may win our bet after all." Dominic smiled and resecured his arm around Athena's waist. With his hand at her side, he could feel her heart beating strong and fast beneath the wool of the pelisse.

"You're a real gentleman," the innkeeper continued, warming to his topic. "You know the price of top cattle like mine." He jerked his head toward the mediocre-looking animals hitched to the carriage. "With these specimens, I say you can catch them inside of an hour."

"An hour!" Athena repeated. Dominic could not tell if she was elated or dismayed.

"They didn't look to be in too much of a hurry," the innkeeper mused. "They were mostly bent on fighting like cats. I'd say they thought they had such a lead on you and your wife here, that there was no need for them to hurry anymore. Like the tortoise and the hare." He laughed to himself. "Yessir, like the tortoise and the hare."

"Thank you for all your help." Dominic bowed before the man could begin talking again. Retaining his grip on Athena, he propelled her across the yard and into the carriage.

"Your wife," she sputtered in annoyance once they were safely in its confines. "Why could I not be your sister?"

He shot her a look of disbelief. "No one in possession of all their faculties would believe that we are related in any other way but marriage," he said in French.

"I speak French," she objected. "Very well. I know we don't resemble each other, but I could have put on an accent if you had warned me."

He continued to regard her in amusement while she sputtered. They lapsed into silence for quite some time.

"Why it is that your parents did not accompany you to Bath?" he inquired at last, hoping to distract her from the anxiety she obviously felt.

She looked out the window at the gray landscape as it rolled by. "They were in the middle of a particularly difficult translation of Herodotus," she replied. "They had been planning to give Cass a Season for years, but time was slipping away, and it did not look as though it was going to happen this year either. She was invited by my aunt Castlereagh to London for the Season, and I was to accompany her, but things became too difficult what with the Corn Law riots and now with the Bonaparte difficulties . . ." Her voice trailed off.

He watched her closely. "Why it is that only Cass was to be given a Season?"

She turned to him, and to his surprise, laughed. "Poor Cass. She never really did fit into the family. Of course many parents would be delighted to have such a lovely, good-natured child, but she isn't very academic, I'm afraid, so I think my parents considered her a bit of a disappointment. I suppose they thought that marriage would be her best option." She looked out the window again and he saw a faint crease form between her fine brows. "I never really thought about it, but it must have been a lot of pressure on her." She sat still in thought for a moment. "I just don't understand why she would feel the need to run away with Wellborne. If she truly wished for the match, there was nothing to impede her."

Fine flecks of rain were beginning to tap softly at the window. Should he tell her? It might only worry her more. No, she deserved to know. He could not tell her everything, but perhaps divulging what he knew about the Wellbornes would exonerate him slightly when the whole truth about him came out. Which it would. He cringed inwardly. That would put a swift period to any tender feelings she felt toward him. He smiled ruefully. After her very matter-of-fact manner last night on the balcony, he wondered if she had tender feelings for him at all.

"Why are you smiling?" she asked.

His head jerked up. "I am thinking that it is only a matter of a short while before we come upon our runaways."

"I hope so." She looked anxiously out into the rain. "Oh, Dominic, I just don't understand." She didn't seem to notice that she had used his Christian name all morning. "Why would she do this? And Sophia?" She turned pleading gray eyes up to his. "Even if Cass is out of her mind and Charles is lost to any finer feelings regarding her reputation and family, Sophia must know the folly of this kind of match. Her going along is hardly going to lend countenance to a marriage made without the knowledge or consent of either of their families!"

He took her hand between his own. It felt so small and thin, encased in delicate Limerick leather. "The Wellbornes have no family," he said gently, watching her reaction carefully.

"Besides their grandmother, you mean. Yes, I do remember that Charles mentioned once that—"

"Their name is not even Wellborne."

"What?"

"Perhaps they are from Scarborough, no one really seems to know for certain. They are actually Charles and Sophia deWit. Their father was a gambler and charlatan." He watched her eyes widen in horror. He moved so that he was sitting beside her in the carriage. "DeWit eventually left his family, and their mother spent her time moving them from lodging to lodging in London without paying the bills. She managed to scrape together enough money to give Miss Wellborne, or Miss deWit, whichever your prefer, a Season in London. She styled herself as an unknown noblewoman from Wallachia, I believe, hoping that her daughter would make an advantageous match. Of course the ruse was quickly discovered.'' Athena had gone pale, but he continued. ''Mrs. deWit died a year ago, and the deWit children seemed to disappear.''

''And their grandmother?'' she whispered, barely able to get the words out.

He shook his head. ''Does not exist. I discovered yesterday that they have not paid the rent on the house in the Westgate Buildings since the first week and the watch was to help the landlord put their things in the street only next week.''

''Why didn't you tell me?'' Her voice was still a plaintive whisper.

''I was not sure. I was not sure until yesterday. And then I saw that you and Sophia did not speak to each other at the Reading-Thrandles' party, so I thought that the friendship between you and her was at an end and the danger was over.''

She sat still for a moment in shock. The words he had said took a long time to translate in her mind. ''You knew that they were adventurers and you did not tell me?'' Her voice rose shrilly. ''How could you go on with your vague warnings that they might not be what they seemed when you knew, you *knew* that they were complete frauds!'' She whipped her hand from between his and balled it into a fist.

''I could not foresee that this would happen,'' he said with infuriating logic.

"You allowed us to be taken in by them! We thought that they were our friends!" she shouted, feeling a small amount of satisfaction at seeing his look of surprise. "And now Cass has been kidnapped by them, and it is all your fault!"

"We will catch up with them very soon, my love. I am certain of it." He took her fist and tried to caress it. "Cass will not have been harmed. She most likely believes that she is still in love with Charles and that they will be married."

"And if she is not ruined or killed or worse, how do you propose to tell her that the man she loves is a fraud?" she snapped. She could hope only that her sister remained deluded and was not even now in a state of terror as she was driven further and further from her family.

"I will take care of everything. You must not worry. I only told you because I thought that you should know."

"I should have known long ago! How do you have all this information? Who are you to be delving into the Wellbornes' past? How do I even know that you are speaking the truth?" But she knew that he was. It all made too much sense. It was not clear why the Wellbornes would want to convince Cass to elope with Charles, but it was definitely even more serious than she had at first conceived. It was not simply her reputation that was in danger, but perhaps her life.

"Athena." Dominic caught her face in his hand. "Do not fall apart. You have been so strong until now. It is not productive for you to fall into hysterics."

She stared at him in irritated surprise. Well of course it was not productive to fall into hysterics. She had never done so in her life for that very reason. But if she should wish to now, it was certainly her right.

"I admit, I should have told you long ago what I knew

about the Wellbornes,'' he continued with a quiet intensity. ''But you must believe me; I did not know the whole until yesterday. I had your best interests at heart and, as I believe you had told me before, I did not think that you would thank me for interfering in your friendship with that family. I did not wish to make false accusations.''

She tried to maintain her anger, but the sincerity of his apology made it difficult. ''How did you find out about them?'' she demanded again, trying not to think about Cass. The long silence was emphasized by the insistent rattling of the rain at the windows.

''Falk told me,'' he said quietly.

''Do you think that it is true?''

''Yes.''

She felt suddenly aware of the cold. ''Will they hurt her?'' She could not look at him. There was something about the kindness and concern in his voice that made her much more prone to hysteria than she had been when she was angry. The inside of the coach windows were misted, but she could see that they were still traveling at a good clip. She tried to take comfort in that.

''No, no,'' he said with reassuring confidence. ''I suspect that they are hoping that Cass will marry Charles and thereby gain respectability and a fortune. Fortune hunters, nothing more.'' He smiled. ''Are you crying?'' he asked suddenly.

''No,'' she lied.

''What is wrong?''

She squeezed her arms more tightly around herself to try to maintain control. ''I'm afraid,'' she whispered.

His arms were around her instantly. ''Don't be. I will take care of you. We will find Cass very soon, and you must think of how upset she will be when she sees that you have been crying. Very likely she still has no idea what has happened.'' His thumb caressed her cheek. ''We will be home in time for a very nice luncheon and a scold from your aunt.'' He obviously meant the words to be teasing, but he said them so softly.

She turned her face up to his. ''I trust you,''

For the merest instant his dark gaze was shuttered. ''Should you?'' he asked, his hand stilling against her cheek.

''Shouldn't I?'' She drew back slightly in his arms.

''Because, my little goddess''—he closed the space between them—''I am going to kiss you, even though you don't like it.''

''But I do like it,'' she murmured huskily when he pulled back from her at last. Merciful heavens, what kind of a wanton was she? The incident on the balcony could be ascribed to simple curiosity, but here she was very nearly sprawled on the seat of the carriage, her bonnet on the floor, wishing he would kiss her again.

''Do you?'' There was a mocking tone in his voice as he kissed down her neck. ''Why?''

''I don't know.'' She laughed in exasperation. ''Must you analyze everything?''

He brushed an escaped curl from her cheek. ''You are learning to think with your heart.''

No. This had nothing to do with love. It was only that she had read about romance and she had been curious to see what all the fuss was about. She was completely in control. Truly. She tried awkwardly to disentangle herself from him. ''I do hate it when you start spouting nonsense, Solage.'' She gave a shaky laugh. ''If one of us doesn't start thinking logically, we would find ourselves in a very awkward position at the next posting house when they open the door to find us making love on the floor of the carriage.''

''Would we?'' He slowly kissed behind her ear.

The thought gave her a warm shiver. ''Yes, if I had

any say in the matter," she said wryly. "Now"—she pushed him away—"I don't believe you would be at all happy with the consequences if we continue. I find it very hard to envision you trekking up to Londonderry to beg my father for my hand." She spoke with heavy sarcasm, but at the notion her heart gave a flutter anyway.

"Or your uncle," Dominic said with a strange expression. He sat up and drew a deep breath with his eyes closed. "How right you are, Miss Montgomery." He tugged down his waistcoat and carefully settled his cuffs. "Perhaps it is better to be somewhat circumspect."

The rain was falling even more heavily, and Athena was glad that its constant roar dulled the edge of the silence inside the carriage. "I hope you don't feel awkward," she said brightly at last. "I suppose we should both be thankful that we are both people who don't take these things very seriously. Not that I have done this before," she amended quickly. She cleared her throat and widened her smile. "But you can trust me that I am not going to advertise what just happened in order to make you propose. I am quite sincere in my wish to never marry."

She shot him a glance and saw that he was slouched in the corner of the carriage, staring into space with his hands steepled in front of him.

"Quite sincere," she repeated desperately. Just as she thought she was going to expire from embarrassment, the coach slowed. The transom popped open and let in a deluge of rainwater.

"Sir," the coachman said urgently, "I can see them!"

"Where?" Athena let down the window and stuck her head out. They were approaching a posting house on the outskirts of Poole. Through the driving rain she could see a figure in a blue cloak disappearing into a closed carriage. "Cass!" she shouted, afraid that her voice would not carry over the noise of the inn, the road, and the rain.

Her sister turned to see where the call had come from, but before she could identify Athena, she was urged into the carriage by her companions.

Solage stood and put his head out the transom. "Spring them," he said grimly.

Chapter Eighteen

"There! There! They turned left," she cried out to the coachman as she hung halfway out of the carriage window.

"I can see them well enough," he replied in annoyance.

"Get back inside the coach, Athena. You'll fall out." She felt Dominic's hands on her hips, and he pulled her bodily back inside the carriage. She gave an unladylike squeak and landed nearly on top of him. "But we must catch them!" She scrambled away from him as fast as she could in the swaying coach. He probably thought she did that on purpose.

"We shall," he said calmly. "Everything is under control."

"Why haven't they stopped? Didn't she see me?" He was unable to provide her with answers, and as the carriage bounced wildly through the streets of Poole, it was easy to believe that everything was not under control. She resisted the urge to put her head out the window

again to see where the Wellbornes' hired coach was going.
Another thought occurred to her. "Surely they know that
we are trying to catch them. If they did not, they would
not be going so fast. But if they do know, they must know
that there is no point in barreling through town." She did
not have a chance to continue her musings as their own
coach gave a sudden lurch that threw them both on the
floor. "Why have we stopped?" she demanded, clamber-
ing back onto the seat.

Dominic looked out the window. "There is a dray
unloading in front of us, and there is not room to pass."

She pressed down the feeling of panic that threatened
to overwhelm her. "Did you see which way they went?
What if we should lose them now? Now when we were
so close?"

He grabbed her hand and squeezed tightly. "We will
find them. They were two hours ahead of us before, do
you remember?"

She nodded silently. It seemed like an age while they
waited for the dray to move ponderously out of their
way. She continued to clutch Dominic's hand. There was
something in its slim, muscular warmth that comforted
her. The coachman turned the carriage in the direction
the Wellbornes' coach had taken.

It was as though they had vanished entirely. The wet
streets were full of carriages and the sidewalks were
crowded with pedestrians; nothing in the scene looked as
though a hired carriage had just run full tilt through the
streets.

"Where are they?" Athena demanded, as though he
could produce them. "They must have turned up another
way while we were waiting." The panic welled up again.
Dominic had said that he would take care of everything,
she reminded herself. The logical part of her brain

reminded her that he had no more control of the situation than she herself did.

"Very strange," Dominic murmured, almost to himself. Athena was not reassured. He stood up and put his head out the transom. "Go to the docks, quickly."

"The docks?" she echoed in confusion.

"Why else would they come to Poole? They plan to leave the country."

"What?" She felt the panic threaten to overwhelm her. "Why?"

Dominic shrugged an expression of helplessness. "It is closer than Gretna Green. No English clergyman would marry your sister to Charles; she has not yet reached her majority. I suppose that the Wellbornes hope to get to Ireland, Scotland, or France."

"But she will have been days without her family! Her reputation will be entirely ruined. It does not matter that Sophia went with them, the gossip will be that she ran off with Charles."

Dominic did not appear to hear her. He had drawn out his pocket watch and was frowning at its face. Athena saw him look anxiously out the window.

"What is the matter?"

"Well," he said reluctantly, "I would not wish to worry you, but I believe that the tide has already turned. We must hope that they were not able to get on a packet." He forced a smile. "Most likely we will find them very frustrated and standing on the dock while their ship sails away without them."

Her throat was too dry to make a reply. She watched anxiously out the window as at last the road turned downhill toward the unmistakable forest of masts and cranes at the waterfront. The whole area was a mass of vans and drays loading and unloading cargo. "We will never get down there. I am going to walk." Before he could protest, she opened the door to the carriage and leapt out into the pouring rain.

He caught up with her before she had gone many steps. "You should not walk around here alone," he chided.

"I am not alone. You are with me," she replied without turning back. Despite her brave front, she was glad to have him beside her as she walked through the clusters of seamen and tradesmen skulking under the scanty protection of the large pyramids of cargo being unloaded. No one dared comment with Solage's arm on her elbow, but she could feel their assessing eyes upon her.

Dominic stopped her under the eaves of the customs house, in front of two sailors dressed in grubby oilskins. "I am looking for a woman," he said.

"Wot's wrong? The one with you ain't good enout?"

"The one I am looking for was wearing a blue cloak and was accompanied by a fair-haired man and woman."

The two men looked at each other in silence for a moment. "I ain't sure ex-zactly who you refer to," one said slyly, his hand creeping forward meaningfully.

"She would have been the prettiest lady here. Perhaps they were bound for France?" He pressed a coin in the eager hand of each.

"The looker!" the sailor feigned remembrance. "Pretty bird, but scolding like a shrew, she was."

"Where are they?" Athena demanded, scanning the traffic along the docks.

"They're gone," the second sailor volunteered. "I saw them get on the dinghy bound for the *Hippocampus*."

"Gone?" she wailed. She pushed her dripping hair out of her eyes and squinted out to where a sloop was starting to unfurl its sails. "But I must get out there!"

"Can you do it?" Several more coins changed hands.

The men looked doubtfully between the rain, the ship, and the Frenchman's purse. "It'll take 'em another ten

minutes to get that main up,'' the shorter one volunteered.
As if that were a signal, both men sprang into action.
One ran down to the end of the pier where a rather
dilapidated skiff bobbed on the waves.

''You'll have to be lively about it,'' the other said,
taking Athena by the elbow and pushing her out into the
rain. ''No boxes? That's right then, don't have time enout
anyways.'' He swung her into the skiff as though she
were a sack of grain and then jumped down after her.
Dominic followed him with an agility that surprised her.
She had the momentary thought that if she had not come
to him this morning, Cass would be lost to her forever.
Perhaps she was anyway, but at least now . . . She clutched
the gunwale as the boat surged over the waves. At least
now they had a chance.

'' 'Eve ho, Squilly,'' the taller sailor said cheerfully,
though the skiff shot through the sea with a speed that
made the raindrops sting painfully. ''Bit o' trouble with
the missus?'' He grinned at Dominic.

''We are delivering a very important message to the
young lady,'' he said grimly. ''It is quite urgent.''

The men exchanged dubious glances. ''It's too late for
'er to get off that boat if you're 'oping she'll come 'ome,''
Squilly said dolefully. ''It might be too late fer you to
get on.''

''Please hurry,'' Athena begged, her eyes on the sails
that continued slowly unfurling, one by one. They were
close enough now that she could see that the ship was
beginning to pick up speed. In a few moments, there
would be no way to catch it.

The sailors bared their teeth to the rain and pulled
harder. ''You'd better shout to them.'' Squilly's companion panted. The main sail was beginning its jerky descent.

Dominic cupped his hands to his mouth and shouted.
Athena tried to add her voice to his, but found that hers

had dwindled into a breathless wheeze. She watched anxiously as there was no response from the sloop.

"There!" On the stern, she saw the white blur of a face turn toward them in the rain. She ripped off her bonnet and waved it frantically. "Wait! Wait!"

There was a bustle of activity and the main sail slackened and began flapping impotently. She held her breath as the skiff slid up to the black hulk of the sloop. "You must let us on," Dominic called out, catching on to a line that trailed from the ship's side.

"What's this?" An officer looked over the railing. "Late passengers? We don't take late passengers. What do you think this is, the London stage? We have to leave with the tide!"

"It's an emergency," Athena begged, vowing that she would climb up the rope to the ship hand over hand if it came to it.

"Government business," Dominic said sternly. "I have orders from Whitehall," he added when they looked down at him skeptically. Athena shot him a covertly admiring glance as a rope ladder was thrown over the side of the ship. That was a clever lie. Once they were found out, they would already be on board. Dominic caught the ladder and steadied it. "Ascend," he said with a wry smile. "I will avert my eyes."

She shot him a darkling glance, gathered her soaking skirts about her, and quickly climbed the ladder. What did a glimpse of leg matter at a time like this? Once she was level with the deck, several sailors grabbed her under the arms and hauled her gracelessly over the railing. "Cass?" she called out, struggling to get her footing. She could hear the sailors grumbling at the delay as they waited for Dominic to climb the ladder, but she forged through the crowd of curious passengers who had gathered to watch their boarding.

"Athena!" She was nearly knocked to the ground by the force of her sister's embrace.

"What has happened? Are you all right?"

"Oh, Athena, everything has gone so terribly wrong! Charles has been just beastly, and I don't wish to marry him at all." Her lower lip went out in a mutinous pout.

Athena took her sister by both arms and resisted the urge to shake her. "Has he harmed you?" she asked urgently.

Cass scowled. "Well, he was very cross." She sniffed. "And he wouldn't hire a private parlor at Blandford Forum *or* Shaftesbury. I had to have my tea in the tap-room! What would Mother say?"

Athena led her sister under the tarp that was strung across the deck. "Where are the Wellbornes now?"

Something behind her own shoulder caught Cass's attention. "Here is Charles now. He'll be very surprised to see you, I should think."

"I should think so too," she muttered, turning around with her hands to her hips.

"Athena!" he gasped. The sudden shocked expression on his face was slightly satisfying. He quickly recovered himself. "And I see you have brought your cavalier."

Athena glanced up to see that Dominic had joined them. The rest of the passengers appeared to have lost interest in the drama and were dispersing to other parts of the ship. The mainsail noisily resumed its descent.

"But you are too late," Charles said quietly.

"Nonsense," she replied with more confidence than she felt. "The ship has sailed, but I am here to chaperone Cass. There can be no question of propriety now."

Charles laughed loudly. "Miss Montgomery, your ideas of chaperonage continue to astound me. You, an unmarried woman, have arrived on a ship after hours of travel, in the sole company of an unmarried man." He clapped her on the shoulder and grinned easily. "Forgive me, but I think it is you who needs a chaperone. My Cass at least had Sophia to lend her countenance."

Athena tried to ignore the flush that she felt creeping up her neck. "Why did you not you simply ask for her hand from her father, like an honorable man?" she demanded. She saw Sophia picking her way across the deck with an umbrella carefully tilted against the steady downpour. She wished that she did not have to face her.

Charles did not seem in the least bit discomposed. "I thought you, of all people, would understand that," he replied. "Cass can make her own decisions. Would not the great Mary Wollstonecraft say that girls should make their own decisions as to marriage rather than let their fathers sell them off like pigs?"

"This has nothing to do with bluestockings, pigs, or even Miss Cassiopeia," Dominic replied darkly. He raised his voice so that Sophia could hear. "It has more to do with the Jamaica Isles Company."

Everyone present stared at Solage in silence. "Mr. and Miss deWit rallied backers for a company that did not exist and then absconded with the money." His eyes narrowed. "The classic case of fraud."

"Falk?" Charles asked calmly.

"DeWit?"

"Bow Street?" Sophia quavered.

"DeWit? Who are the deWits?" Cass's voice was growing peevish. "Athena, I do hope you explained to Auntie that I was going to France to get married rather than Gretna Green as I had originally thought."

"How was I supposed to know where you were going?" Athena retorted irritably. "You told me Gretna Green and Solage said this boat was going to France! I haven't a clue where we are going, and you can trust that Auntie Montie has even less of one!" She watched anxiously as the city and the bobbing skiff slipped further and further away.

Dominic seemed to collect himself first. "Falk informed me," he replied to Charles. "He is involved in the Ministry of Commerce. You both face serious charges of fraud."

"In England," Charles reminded him with a careless shrug. Athena's eyes again darted to the coastline. England was growing mistily indistinct in the rain. "We'll disappear fairly well in France. Plenty of English remain there; what is three more?" He turned to Athena and smiled wryly. "Your cavalier accuses us of fraud," he said. "But at least I care for Cass. I cared for you too, of course, but you're a bit too prim for a wrong 'un like me." His laugh was self-deprecatory "I gave it a try though, you know I did! I guess all will be forgiven once we're all related though, eh?"

Sophia rolled her eyes expressively. "Do stop, Charles. You're giving me the headache. You know Cass's family will have the marriage annulled."

"No, really, it will all work out perfectly," he insisted. "I will marry Cass, Athena will marry her cavalier, and then he, being that he's all right and tight with Castlereagh, will get us out of this fix."

"You know my uncle?" Athena demanded in amazement. She looked up at Dominic

"He works for your uncle!" Charles exclaimed. "You didn't tell her, Solage? Shame on you! Who is the fraud here? I went after both girls fair and square. You took the easy road and courted the plain one just to cuddle up to Castlereagh."

"You know my uncle?" she repeated, anger creeping into her voice. Why didn't he tell her? After everything they had been through? Those kisses? Was it really . . . ? She thought of Solage's friendship with Falk, the mysterious trips to London, and the times when he had said that he could not explain how he knew certain things. And the list. That damn list! She turned on him in fury. "You lied to me about everything!"

He held up his palms in protest. "Athena, I could not—"

"Get away from us." Cass grabbed her sister's hand and stepped in front of her. "You are an encroaching toad-eater who only pretended to like Athena to further your career. I think you are detestable!"

"It looks like the wedding is off," Sophia grumbled. She drew a pistol from her reticule and leveled it at Solage with an expression of irritation. "I'm sorry, but you don't really serve a purpose anymore."

"Sophia!" Athena turned to her friend with a gasp and made a move to grab her wrist. In the instant that she turned, there was a faint splash, and Dominic was gone.

Chapter Nineteen

"Gone!" Charles whistled, as the four of them pressed themselves to the railing and peered into the black water. He was silent for a moment and then shrugged. "Pity. If he only would have married you, Athena, things might have worked out rather well."

"What a rude thing to say," Cassiopeia protested. "It isn't as though he chose death rather than marry Athena. Well, not exactly anyway."

Sophia put the pistol back into her reticule. "Well"— she sighed—"it probably would have misfired anyway. I think the powder got damp in the dingy."

Athena did not hear them. She stood staring into the darkness of the water. The rain relentlessly spattered its heaving surface as it slid by into a tumbled rut of wake. She felt Charles's arm go around her shoulders and pulled away.

"Look," he said kindly, "Sophie would never have brought herself to shoot him. She didn't mean for him to do that. He's probably all right. He might be able to swim to shore.'' He squinted at the dim gray shoreline. ''Well, maybe not, but maybe a fishing boat will pick him up. Yes, or that boat that brought you out here. That's it, the boat that brought you here will pick him up. He'll be all right, you'll see.''

''Besides,'' Sophia added, pulling her toward the stairs going below decks, ''I don't believe you would have wanted him for a beau anyway. Not when he lied to you like that. Honestly, Athena, I thought he must have told you. Charles would not have said anything if he thought Solage was keeping it a secret.''

Athena stared at them in disbelief. Were these people insane? Did they cordially offer to shoot you one moment and then comfort you the next?

''They're very odd, aren't they?'' Cass whispered as they were ushered down into the ship. ''I spent all day with them. I am quite positive that I don't wish to marry Charles, except that I might hurt his feelings.''

Sophia opened the door to a small cabin. ''Go on, Charles. I will join you in a moment.'' She ushered the sisters into the room with a defeated gesture. ''This will have to do for the both of you. We had intended it for Cass and me, but I suppose there will be room enough for me in Charles's cabin.'' She sighed tiredly. ''We can't afford to hire another cabin, unfortunately. Bath was much more expensive than I thought it would be, and we really won't have a groat until Charles and Cass marry. I suppose it is too much to hope that you would have any blunt.'' Sophia suddenly looked older than her years, and very careworn.

''How could you do this to me?'' Athena's voice sounded hoarse, as though she had not used it in years.

''Oh, Athena, don't you understand? We have no one to look after us, Charles and I. Solage was right, we did make up a fraud scheme. But we only approached the men who had lifted a fortune from our father at the tables.'' She lifted her chin and continued quickly. ''I know that that does not make it right. But things are going to be different now. Surely your family will get used to the idea of Charles married to Cass, and then they can live quite comfortably. I know running away was the wrong thing to do, but it did seem like the only way.'' She looked pleadingly at Athena. ''And they do love each other, you know.''

Cass made a funny noise in her throat, but Sophia had pressed her fingers to her forehead and did not appear to hear. ''I'm so sorry this has happened,'' she said to the floor. ''I never meant for it to get this complicated.'' She looked up and Athena saw that there were tears trembling in her eyes. ''I'm very sorry for Solage. You know I never meant . . . Well anyway . . .'' She shook herself. ''I just wanted you to know that I completely understand that you will never wish to speak to me again, even when I am your sister-in-law, but you have been a very dear friend to me. Maybe my only friend,'' she added with a sad half laugh.

She turned to Cass. ''Charles will make you a fine husband. Things will be different from now on. He is a true gentleman, and I think that you will be very happy together. Thank you for falling in love with him. It gave us our first hope for a life of respectability.'' The silence in the room was made more obvious by the mournful creak of the ship. Sophia ducked her head to hide her tears and stepped out of the room. At the last moment, she turned back. ''I never would have shot him. You know that, don't you?''

The door shut with a click and the two sisters sat in silence.

''I feel terrible.'' Cass sighed after a long moment. ''I

can never break off the engagement now. Not when it means so much to them.'' She stood up and began to pace the cramped room. ''I suppose I will *grow* to love Charles.''

Athena only shrugged carelessly. Dominic had abandoned them. He had lied to her about who he was and what he did, and then he had abandoned them to people he knew were adventurers and schemers. So much for all his requests for her trust. Perhaps he was dead. She squeezed her eyes tightly closed to block out the idea. It was not very far to the skiff. He might have been able to swim that far. If he could swim. The topic had not come up on the starlit balcony or the carriage.

Cass sat her down on the narrow berth. ''I feel certain that Solage is all right. I know you are worried, but I really do think that he could not have drowned.'' Her face brightened. ''After all, no one forced him to jump off the ship. Surely he would not have done so if he could not swim!''

''He left us of his own free will.''

''Yes.'' She nodded vigorously. Her smile fell. ''Yes,'' she repeated darkly. ''Not really very chivalrous, was it?''

''Not very.'' Charles's words rung in her ears. Dominic had only pretended to care for her to forward his own political career. He was as bad as Charles himself— hoping to win himself a wife whose connections benefited him. But who had said Solage ever wanted her for his wife? She was vaguely aware that her nails were digging into her palms. ''Why does Sophia think that you are in love with Charles?'' she asked her sister suddenly.

Cass's pretty face crumpled into a pathetic expression of guilty remorse. ''I . . .'' She cleared her throat. ''I am not sure.'' She stood up and took a turn around the small cabin. ''It is most likely because he told her that I was.''

She smiled weakly. "Because I told him that I was." She hung her head. "I shouldn't have, I know. But Auntie said that he had proposed to you and that you had said no."

Athena was jerked out of her reverie. "How would she know? Why would that matter?"

"She was watching you in the garden with him." She gave an expressive shrug. "Apparently she is very adept at interpreting pantomime. Anyway"—she gave a tight, regretful smile—"I thought that if I told him I loved him, he would feel obliged to marry me."

"But you don't love him." She couldn't concentrate on Cass and her love troubles. Not when Dominic could be dead. No. He couldn't be. He just couldn't be. She pressed her sweaty palms together and forced herself to breathe in and out to the rhythmic repetition of the words in her head.

"No." Her sister drew the word out slowly. "But I was beginning to get a little worried that no one would ask me at all, and then I would have to go home to Mama and Papa at the end of the Season, and you would stay on with Auntie Montie, and everyone would be disappointed in me. Like they always are."

"I don't understand." Nothing was making sense. It didn't seem like anyone was using honest methods to get what they wanted. She thought of the look on Dominic's face when Charles had exposed him. If he wasn't dead, he deserved to be. Her throat felt as though it were closing up.

Cass made a frustrated gesture and slouched onto the berth. "I was always the great disappointment of the family. I was never clever like you." When Athena didn't reply, she frowned and crumpled further. "I saw that Charles was a bit sweet on you, and I was quite irritated because it would be just so awful if you were to get *married* on top of being clever, and I would be left with nothing.'' She ignored Athena's noise of protest. ''And of course I did have hopes for Solage myself, but it became obvious that *he* was in love with you too!'' She laughed ruefully. ''So when you turned down Charles's offer, I thought that perhaps, he could be convinced to marry me.''

''Cass!''

''I know. Well, anyway, it was my idea to elope. It seemed best to get the whole thing over with before Charles changed his mind. I really did think that we were going to Gretna, so don't think that I deceived you on purpose. But I suppose France will serve as well.'' Her voice took on a fatalistic tone.

''You plan on going through with it?'' Athena asked in horror.

''What can I do? My reputation is ruined, the Wellbornes are dead set on the idea now, because I told them the fact that Mama and Papa had settled twenty thousand pounds on me, and now we are trapped in a boat bound for Cherbourg.'' Her expression dared her sister to deny the truth of her statements.

''Why didn't you marry Lord Aston or one of your other beaux? Why did it have to be Charles?'' The whole conversation was inane and was beginning to make her head ache. He couldn't be dead. He couldn't be dead. Perhaps he was even now shivering on the skiff that had brought them on board the *Hippocampus,* feeling nothing but relief at being rid of her. It must be the motion of the ship on the waves that made her feel ill, because she was glad to be rid of him, too. How awful it might have been if Charles had not divulged Dominic's secret. She might have married him in ignorance! She reminded herself again that no one had ever mentioned marriage. The swell of the waves made her feel very ill indeed.

Cass had been staring at the wooden beams of the ceiling. "My other beaux didn't ask to marry me, and he did." There was a strange, resigned bitterness in her voice, but she stood up with a pretense of cheerful resignation. "Well, I daresay I will learn to care for him." She squeezed her hands tightly together. "But I did think this morning that I truly hated him. He was very impatient with me when we were trying to leave. I couldn't help it that I was not quite ready, and I really did have to make sure that I had packed my yellow gloves, which of course turned out to be in the bottom of the trunk all along, and then I did make him turn around when we were half an hour down the road, because I had left my pillow behind, and you know I can't sleep without my own pillow."

Athena could not repress a faint, sad smile.

"And then he would not hire a private parlor no matter how much I said that he must. It really was quite shocking to have to stay in the taproom while they changed the horses. And those horses, I declare, Athena, I am not in the least surprised that you caught up with us. Charles would hire the most down-at-heel creatures you ever saw. I know they haven't got money, but really, to see him haggle with the hostlers and try to wiggle out of paying tolls and such, it was quite humiliating. But"—she shrugged—"I suppose he might improve once he is not so poor."

"Don't marry him. He has lied to you. How can you love or respect him when he lied to you?" There was a sharp pain in her side that would not go away.

"I haven't any choice"—she raised hopeful eyes to her sister—"have I?"

"Of course you do. We shall just have to tell the Wellbornes that you have changed your mind."

Cass looked at her as though she had lost her mind. "Sophia threatened to shoot Monsieur Solage! No matter what she says, I am not at all sure that she would not have done it.''

Athena chewed the inside of her cheek for a moment. ''Then we shall have to escape,'' she said confidently at last. She could take care of herself and Cass on her own. She didn't need him.

''Escape? We're on a boat!''

Athena thought for a long moment. ''Perhaps we can disguise ourselves as other passengers.'' Cass looked at her doubtfully. ''Or, when we arrive at the docks, we'll jump off the lighter that takes the passengers to the docks.''

''I don't like that idea at all,'' her sister said quickly.

Athena fell silent. Her thoughts were crowded by an insistent ache. No, she would not think about out. Later, when they were safe, she could nurse her wounds, but now, there were more important things. ''I have it,'' she said quickly.

Dominic pulled himself slowly out of the water. *Dieu*, but it was cold. He forced his cold fingers to wrap around the stiff line, prickly with hemp fibers, and hauled his weight up the side of the ship. In the wind, it felt even colder than it had in the water. He focused on the length of rope ahead of him. It would be dark soon and the cold wind had driven the sloop's few passengers belowdecks. He hauled himself up another foot. It was hard to know what it was more important to not think about: the debilitating cold or Athena. The Wellbornes, deWits, whatever they called themselves, were obviously desperate. He clenched his teeth to keep them from chattering.

''Quel idiot,'' he muttered to himself. They were desperate, but perhaps he should have gambled against that desperation. But his only thought when he had seen the

pistol Sophia held was that he was endangering Athena.
With him out of the way, there was no reason the Wellbornes would not continue with their plan. Athena could
just become part of their bargaining power to the Montgomery family. Both she and Cass were valuable to them.
When he stood between the Wellbornes and their goals,
they certainly would have killed him, but they might have
hurt Athena as well.

He stifled a grunt of exertion and pulled himself up the
last few inches. The deck was empty except for a few
sailors who went about their duties with the collars of
their peacoats turned up and their caps screwed tightly
down over their eyes. Perhaps they had killed her anyway.
They were bizarre people, raised on the fringe of society
where deception and desperation were part of normal life.
He decided to concentrate on the cold.

He dropped to the deck with a soft, wet splat and cringed
at the agonizing pain that shot through his frozen feet.
No one on deck reacted. He straightened his limp cravat
and strolled the length of the deck, hoping that the creak
of the sails and the rhythmically flapping lines disguised
the undeniable squish in each of his steps.

"My dear sir! What happened?" A porter at the bottom
of the companionway looked up in shock.

"Ah, just a slight accident. Nothing to worry about."
He smiled and shrugged. And prayed.

"You will wish to change immediately, of course. Shall
I show you to your cabin?" The confused frown deepened
on the young man's face.

"Not at all. I can find it on my own." He waved
a negligent hand and continued down the hall, hoping
desperately that the man would continue on his business.
He paused at a door at the end of the narrow hallway and
looked casually over his shoulder. *Diantre!* The porter

was still standing helpfully at the foot of the stairs. He turned the handle and pushed into the cabin.

His entrance was met with a faint scream. A maid held up her mistress's dress in front of her like a shield. She was obviously there to straighten the cabin while her employer was down at dinner.

"So sorry, mademoiselle," he murmured, preparing to retreat, but hoping to gain a little time so that the porter might leave. "I seem to have entered the wrong room," he added unnecessarily with a grin.

"What happened to you?" She eyed him curiously from behind the gown.

"I met with a slight accident. Is it dinnertime? I had no idea it was so late." He pulled out his pocket watch and examined its immobile hands.

"Yes, they've all gone down to dinner. I hope you plan to change before you go, sir." She giggled.

Everything was quiet outside the cabin. Perhaps it was safe to remove himself. "Indeed I shall," he brushed ineffectually at his jacket, "I seem to have formed quite a puddle. And then to make the matters worse, I am unable to find my cabin. It was right next door to one occupied by a pretty blond woman who was traveling with her brother. You would not happen to remember the passengers?"

"Aye," she said. "There aren't many passengers aboard. France isn't the most popular destination right now. But you're French, aren't you?"

"Yes. So you remember the brother and sister?" he pressed.

"Aye, but I don't know their room. I think it was at the other end of the hall." She giggled again. "But you'd better ask the porter where your room is, sir. You gave me quite a fright, bursting in like you did. Who knows who you might walk in on if you just pop into cabins all higgildy piggildy.''

''Very good advice.'' Solage bowed deeply and let himself out of the room. The hallway was mercifully empty. He tiptoed down to the end, a self-mocking smirk creeping to his lips as he looked back down the hall to see a neat double row of wet footprints. So much for being stealthy.

He pressed his ear against the door closest to the stairs leading up to the deck. Silence. In the second, there was the faint sound of a valet singing to himself. It was a rather shocking ditty about a girl named Peg; he remembered hearing it on the docks. He leaned against the third door, concentrating on the sounds within.

The maid had been right, the schooner was not carrying very many passengers. Most of the doors along the hallway were unlocked and obviously unoccupied. He had hoped to hear Athena's voice in one of the cabins, but his luck appeared to have run out. Had she and Cassiopeia convivially gone down to dinner with the Wellbornes? Perhaps Charles and Sophia had locked them up somewhere else, rather than in their cabin.

A hand clapped him heavily on the shoulder. ''What's going on here?'' the first mate demanded. Yes, his own luck had definitely run out. Over the man's shoulder was the anxious face of the porter who had seen him earlier. ''Are you a passenger?''

''In a manner, yes.''

''What is that supposed to mean? Either you are or you aren't. Look, I am going to have to take you to the captain. We can't have these kind of havey-cavey goings-on with strange people listening at the passengers' doors. Strange, wet people,'' he amended, removing his hand from Solage's shoulder and examining his damp palm with distaste.

''Certainly. Take me to the captain, if you please.''

Very well. It might have been heroic to have rescued Athena single-handedly, but perhaps now was the time to involve the authorities.

In his stateroom, the captain looked nonplussed. "Do I have this correct? You work for Whitehall for Lords Falk and Castlereagh, who are not here to vouch for you. You have warrants of arrest for two of my passengers, but they were lost when you jumped overboard because one of them threatened to shoot you." His toe tapped impatiently. "Not only are these two passengers wanted for investigation into some financial scheming, but they have kidnapped a young lady who to the untrained eye, appeared to come aboard this boat entirely of her own free will?" The edge of sarcasm in his voice grew sharper. "In order to rescue this young lady, you held up the departure of my vessel, but have not paid your passage because, of course, your purse is at the bottom of Poole Bay. That is a fascinating story." He took a turn around the room with his hands locked behind his back. "Where is this young lady now?"

"I was hoping that you would help me to find her, sir." Solage forced his voice to remain civil.

"Moore, ask Mr. and Miss Wellborne to attend us here, if you please." Captain Sturges resumed his pacing. His eyes narrowed as they turned again to Solage. "And ask their guest to accompany them."

Dominic leaned against the bulkhead of the stateroom with what he hoped was an air of casual disinterest. Where could they have gone? Had they harmed her? If they had, he would make them pay. His jaw was beginning to ache from clenching.

"You are French, eh, Solage?" the captain asked after a long moment.

"I am."

He grunted. "You are aware that we are at war with

France?'' His bristly gray eyebrows rose slightly in derision.

Solage stared him down. He was in no mood to explain his mixed heritage. Besides, he had no proof of that either. Athena would arrive in a moment and everything would be sorted out. His mouth twisted slightly. She would be the one rescuing him, from the looks of it. Or would she? His mouth stilled. The look on her face when Charles had announced his perfidy . . . No, there was no way now to explain that his love for her had nothing to do with Castlereagh.

''Captain''—Moore burst into the room—''the Wellbornes are coming up. But, sir''—his ginger brows crushed together—''no one can find the girl.''

''What girl?''

''The girl that came on board with the Wellbornes. The one that was''—he darted a glance at Solage—''kidnapped. We've looked everywhere for them. She and the other young lady are gone!''

Chapter Twenty

Athena heard them coming. No, it was too soon for anyone to be thinking of unloading the cargo. They were searching for something. She pulled herself into an even tighter ball and tried to quiet her raspy breathing. The trunk was large, but of course it had not been designed to contain a slightly taller-than-average woman. She wondered how Cass was faring.

"They can't be in here," a voice whined.

"Cap'n said to look everywhere," a second voice replied. "And there ain't many more places to look."

"They probably jumped over and drowned. It would be just like a woman to do that. Figuring all is lost and such like that." There was a pause punctuated by the sound of crates being dragged across the floor of the hold. "Was she really being kidnapped?"

"I don't know. I don't care. More than likely it is some cock-and-bull story made up by that Frenchie. All I know is that there isn't anyone here."

Athena felt as though she were choking. There was a narrow crack where the halves of the trunk met, but it didn't seem to let in much air. She hoped Cass wasn't suffocating. With some reservations she had decided to lock Cass into her trunk, so that it would not arouse suspicion. She could not fasten her own shut from the inside, of course, but she wondered now if her sister had enough air.

"You don't think they could be hiding *inside* the luggage, do you?"

There was a pause. "Maybe. But think of the roar if we go looking through the passenger's gewgaws."

"They're probably locked up all right and tight anyway." She held her breath and squeezed her eyes tightly closed as someone kicked the trunk.

"Oy! That lock's been forced!" She knew it was over.

"So it has! But it's awfully small for . . ." The men silenced, as though they suddenly realized that they were overheard. She clenched herself as small as she could be in a fruitless bracing for the inevitable.

"It's her!" She felt the rush of air as they threw the lid open and could not help drawing in a deep, gasping breath. The two sailors took her by the arms and hauled her unceremoniously out of the trunk. "Are you the kidnapped miss?"

"I . . . yes. Yes, I am." Maybe they would not feel the need to search further.

"No she ain't," the younger of the two protested. "They said the kidnapped one was pretty. This must be the other one. Not,"—his eyes widened as he realized what he had said—"that you ain't just fine lookin', miss," he amended.

"Shut your stupid face," his companion recommended tersely, as he began throwing open the lids of other trunks large enough to conceivably hold a person. "Here it is.

This one's been forced too." He opened the trunk with a flourish and dragged out a coughing Cassiopeia.

"Why are you ladies hiding down here?" the young sailor demanded. "You could have suffocated in them trunks."

"We were going to be unloaded with the cargo," Cass retorted indignantly as she was escorted up the stairs. "Athena said that people escaped from France during the Terror by hiding in trunks aboard ships."

"Well, we're going *to* France, not *from* it." The sailor laughed boisterously. Athena narrowed her eyes at him and lifted her chin as she was led ignominiously up the stairs.

All eyes turned as they were triumphantly escorted into the captain's stateroom. Dominic suppressed a sigh of relief. She was alive.

" 'Ere they are. They were hiding in the cargo hold. Found some bigish trunks, chucked the clothes out the porthole, and bedded down for the night. Hoped to be unloaded nice as you please when we arrive in Cherbourg."

Both women were crumpled and dirty, but Athena held her head defiantly high, as though she were on trial instead of him. Her eyes swept the room and lit on him. She gave a choked gasp and grabbed her sister's arm. "Dominic . . ." she breathed. Her gray eyes were wide and dilated. "Thank heaven you weren't drowned." He staggered backwards as she flung herself into his arms. "My darling, I thought—I couldn't bear to think—But you—How did you . . ." The rest of her incoherencies were lost in his cravat. She felt so warm against the cold clamminess of his wet clothes. He inhaled deeply to fill himself with the scent of her. Oh yes, this was worth a dunking in the sea.

"How dare you put yourself in such danger!" She held him out at arm's length and looked as though she were going to shake him like a naughty child.

"Athena!" Cass exclaimed, dragging out the word to express her shock. He felt the rest of the people in the room staring.

In a moment, he saw her relief turn to anger and then congeal into a cold mask of fury. Her eyes were instantly reserved and cool. "Forgive me," she murmured and stepped away. He crossed his arms to try to retain the feeling of her closeness.

"Do you know this man?" the captain demanded.

There was a moment of silence in which Athena looked him directly in the eye. "No," she said slowly at last. "I am not at all sure that I do."

Everyone in the room seemed slightly stunned by her response. "Well"—the captain cleared his throat at last—"then I don't suppose you should be throwing yourself at him." He walked to the top of the room and stood with his feet wide apart. "Now. I want this nonsense sorted out," he snapped. "I have better things to do with my time than play nursemaid to a bunch of lunatics full of outrageous stories." He crossed his arms over his broad barrel chest and scowled at everyone in the room.

"First, there is a ridiculous Frenchman who goes leaping on and off of ships at will and accusing decent people of conspiring to kidnap. For all we know, he is a French spy."

"No, he isn't," Sophia put in quickly. "I thought he might be too at first, but he is not."

"Not a spy," Captain Sturges echoed.

"Not in the least."

"Then what is he?" The captain did not seem to see fit to address him himself, but examined him up and down as though he were an interesting but distasteful specimen.

"He works for the Foreign Minister," Charles supplied.

"Oh!" The captain looked stunned. An ingratiating smile slowly crossed his face. "I don't understand. With Castlereagh, you say? Well, well, well, that is another matter entirely!" The captain crossed the room and shook his hand heartily. "You understand my suspicion, of course. Policy, my friend, policy. Can't be too careful! Especially in these dangerous times!" He laughed loudly and slapped him on the back. "Damn man! You're soaking wet! Get this man some clothes! He'll die of a chill!"

"You are too kind," Dominic replied dryly.

"Now." The captain whirled on the rest of the party. "Now I understand. The culprits in this whole sinister business are Mr. and Miss Wellborne!" He struck out with an accusing forefinger. "After defrauding innocent Englishmen with their financial scheme, they kidnapped these young ladies."

"No, just me," Cass piped up. She stepped forward and lay her hands confidentially on the captain's arm. "And do you know? I think it was me who kidnapped them. You see, I convinced Charles to elope with me. He was the one who insisted on bringing Sophia, for respectability you know." She released the stunned man and went to where the Wellbornes stood. "I'm sorry. It was wrong of me to get your hopes up. About my twenty thousand pounds and all. But I am afraid that I can not marry you after all, Charles."

Dominic felt an unexpected twinge of sympathy at Wellborne's stunned expression. "But, Cass," Wellborne protested weakly, "you said . . ." His voice trailed off and he sat down limply on the settee behind him. He looked genuinely distraught. So Charles cared for Cass after all. He hadn't given him credit for that.

"Look," the captain protested. "I don't have the time to be listening to this farcical nonsense. I will not allow this kind of uproar on my ship. Are there any arrests to be made? We have no French spy, and now, apparently, no kidnapping. If anyone has caused any trouble, it would appear to be this young lady.'' He indicated Cassiopeia. He then turned to Dominic and put on a sudden sycophantic smile. ''Tell me, Solage, what should I do? What would Castlereagh do?''

''Well . . .'' Dominic rubbed his chin thoughtfully to cover a smile. ''I do not think that he would arrest the girl. As she is his niece.''

''Niece!'' the captain fairly screamed. ''Is this some kind of joke on me? I will not tolerate any more of this! Clap those Wellborne people in irons. At least I am sure that they have done something wrong.''

''No, don't.'' Athena stepped forward. ''You are letting yourself become overwrought.'' She spoke so calmly and looked so composed, even though he could see that her wrinkled, dirty green-and-white gown had only two of the three tapes tied and nearly all of the hem ripped off. Something in her soothing voice produced a feeling of serenity in him. Ah, the unconquerable Athena.

''It was terribly unfortunate that you have become involved in this, but I believe that everything is under control. With your permission, once we are in France, I will see that the passage for both Monsieur Solage and myself is paid. Mr. and Miss Wellborne will accompany us back to England on the next packet.'' He saw her look steadily at the Wellbornes until they dropped their heads in mute compliance. ''And once there we will sort out this business that they are accused of.'' She turned back to the captain, who was regarding her with undisguised admiration. ''So you see, there is nothing else for you to do. Except perhaps''—she cast Dominic a careless glance—''some dry clothes for that man.''

He looked around the room. Sophia looked resigned,

Charles pensive. Cassiopeia anxiously watched Charles, but the pugnacious rise to her chin suggested that she would not attempt to resume the engagement. Yes, they all thought that everything was fairly well settled. He glanced at Athena's forbidding profile. His fight was only beginning.

Chapter Twenty-one

Looking strangely unlike himself in his borrowed sailor's garb, Dominic sternly approached her where she stood with the captain. He looked ready to do battle. Very well. If that was what he wished, she had a few choice words she would like to express regarding his notions of honor, trust, and honesty.

He addressed himself to Captain Sturges. "If you do not object, I would like to speak privately with Miss Montgomery."

The man started. "Not at all!" he exclaimed jovially. "By all means. Make yourselves entirely at home. We shall arrive in Cherbourg in a few hours." He lowered his voice slightly. "I do hope that you will remember to mention me favorably when this incident is reported to Castlereagh. Great man, Castlereagh." He bobbed his head hopefully.

"Of course." Solage bowed and propelled Athena quickly out of the room.

"And what if I object?" Athena asked sharply.

"Please do not." He was standing entirely too close for her to refuse. "The rain has stopped. Would you like to walk on the deck?" When she did not reply, he took her by the arm and led her up the companionway. It took a moment for her eyes to adjust to the darkness above deck. The shadowy shapes of the sailors moved about with a sureness that seemed unearthly on the undefined hulk of the ship.

"The *Hippocampus*," he said, looking up to the mast tipping back and forth above them in the blackness. "It is Greek for sea horse. But of course you know that."

There was a long silence. "Did you wish to speak about the Greek language?" she asked.

He gave a little laugh and shot her a rueful grin. "I don't know where to begin, Athena."

"I had supposed that you would begin by making elaborate excuses as to why you lied to me." She drew a deep breath of the sea air. It smelled like the cold dampness before a snow. She wrapped her arms around her body and waited for him to respond.

"I did not lie to you," he said simply.

She stopped dead. "I am going back down to Cass. I don't believe we have anything to discuss."

He caught her arm. "I did not lie, but I did deceive you," he said tensely. "I only wanted . . ." His exhaled breath seemed to deflate him. He led her over to the side of the deck and then let her go and leaned both arms on the railing. "Where should I start? My sister married an Englishman who was the part of the entourage of the English ambassador to France. When I expressed an interest in politics, he set me up with Falk."

They both stared into the darkness toward where the black plane of the sea melded seamlessly into the cloudy night. Not a single star was visible through its heavy blanket. It was as though they were speeding through a strange, silent void. She shivered in her gown, still damp from the rain.

"I am half English, if you recall, and I was not happy with the way things were in France. I thought that England would be more amenable to my way of thinking." They stood in silence for a moment, listening to the labored groaning of the ship as it cut through the waves.

"I know your uncle quite well," he continued softly, almost to himself. She had to lean closer to hear him. "I have served as Falk's courier for the Committee since last autumn when his gout necessitated his retiring to Bath."

He seemed to be waiting for her to reply. "Why didn't you say something from the first?" Strangely, she didn't feel very angry any more. Somehow the darkness and the silence beyond the sounds of the ship on the water had leeched it away. There was only a kind of sadness left.

"I couldn't," he said simply, still looking out into the void. "I was acting only as a courier and an assistant to Falk. They were not my secrets to tell."

She watched his strong profile for a moment, but he did not turn to her. "I understand that now. It was wrong of me to have accused you of deception. I know that it is sometimes necessary." She felt a heaviness in her chest that made it difficult to breathe. But why did his role as the Continental flirt have to include breaking her heart? "Well," she said briskly, "your duty to Castlereagh certainly did not include jaunts across the countryside, pistol-waving adventurers, or plunges into the sea." She gave a short laugh that came out sounding unlike a laugh at all. She stabbed out her hand for him to shake. "I can never thank you enough for what you did today. Cass doesn't seem to realize the danger she was in, but you have saved her from a life of misery."

He took her hand but did not shake it. He caressed it slowly, and when she tried to pull it away, he brought it to his cheek. "My duty to Castlereagh also did not include a kiss stolen on a starlit balcony or a very pleasurable carriage ride." The one-sided smile that crossed his face made her throat constrict painfully.

"Athena . . ." He pressed a kiss into her palm. "I know you think that I have"—he searched for the word—"courted you, pursued you, attempted to seduce you"—the self-mocking smile appeared reluctantly—"in order to curry favor with Castlereagh. But you must see that it is exactly the opposite." For the first time since they had come up on deck, he turned to look directly at her. She had to remind herself to continue to draw her breath.

"Castlereagh will call me out when he finds that I have had the impudence to fall in love with you."

The knot in her chest fell limply into her stomach. She drew herself up stiffly. "Monsieur Solage. There is no need for histrionics. We are two adults who—who enjoyed each other's company on a—a few occasions." Why was her voice shaking? She cleared her throat ruthlessly. "Please remember that I am far beyond the age of compromising and that there is no need for anyone to ever know how much time we spent alone in each other's company. There is no need for misguided gallantry."

She gave a surprised gasp when he pulled her into his arms. "My prim little bluestocking," he murmured fondly into her hair. "Can't you understand that I have fallen in love with you, even though it was not logical or convenient or well thought-out?"

She made a little laughing noise of protest against the rough wool of his borrowed peacoat. "How am I to believe a man who is well known for his flattery?" she asked, half chiding.

He abruptly stepped back and held her at arm's length.

"Athena," he said sternly, "you know I am sincere. This is nothing like—*enfin,* I will show you." He stepped back to her and caught her to him in a single motion. She knew he was going to kiss her, but somehow the reality of it unstrung any strength she had.

"Shall we marry on the way back to Bath, or would you prefer to wait?" he asked breathlessly at last. "Perhaps the captain of the *Hippocampus* . . ."

"Marry?" she repeated stupidly.

"Of course we will marry. Don't you wish it? Oh, my little goddess, do not say that you are still opposed to marriage. You would not make me suffer like that, would you?" He took her cheeks in both his hands and searched her eyes anxiously.

"No," she said in a small voice, "I am not so very opposed."

"Then you will?"

"If you wish." She felt suddenly shy. Could he be sincere? She felt as though her heart were trying to squeeze its way out through her ribs.

"Oh yes"—he laughed softly—"I wish." He grinned. "I will return to Bath a conquered man."

"Don't be ridiculous," she said bracingly, but her fingers crept up to touch his lips. "We are a very good match indeed. My uncle was always encouraging me to mix in political circles, and my aunt had high hopes of me making a diplomatic alliance with one of their friends. I told her at the time that she would have to transfer her hopes to Cassiopeia, but . . . just think of the literary people we can invite to our salons!" she interrupted herself excitedly. "I'm frightfully Whiggish in my tastes, Dominic. Our house will be in a constant uproar, I'm afraid. Can you imagine dinner parties with Countess Bledloe and Lord Oxbridge both attending? We shall have to replace the broken dishes every week!'' She laughed delightedly.

"I look forward to it." He drew her to him again. "As long as our time is not spent entirely in improving our minds and gaining new knowledge." He placed a slow kiss behind her ear and lowered his voice to a whisper. "We must honor Aphrodite, my dear, and leave a little time for love."

"I always knew." Mrs. Beetling nodded sagely. "I said to Celia from the very first that she had her eye on him."

Lady Battford took another sip of water and made a face. "I shall never finish a whole glass of this nasty stuff. I do wish it was fashionable to drink orgeat or ratafia or something rather than this." Her eyes followed Monsieur and Madame Solage as they slowly circled the Pump Room. They were talking avidly with Falk as Dominic pushed him in his Bath chair. "Indeed, all that talk about remaining single, it was fustian. A pretty, clever girl like that does not grow up to be a spinster."

"Indeed no. My Celia could have caught Solage, if she'd had a mind to, but I am not sure I would fancy having her marry a foreigner. Even if he is with the Foreign Ministry. No, Athena Montgomery made him her conquest from the start. I suppose he prefers clever women. I hear that is all the fashion on the Continent. I daresay it is a good match. They are both frightfully bookish." She raised her lorgnette to examine the laughing couple.

"I know. Not at all the thing really."

Mrs. Beetling shuddered. "Their wedding service was simply filled with classical readings. It was practically pagan. Shocking of course, but old Louisa Montgomery indulges her.'' She shook her head.

''My Anne says that they plan to set up house in London,'' Lady Battford volunteered. ''Castlereagh's pleased as punch of course. I hear it took him a while to get used to the idea—both of them are staunch Whigs—but he bent in the end of course. They will hold some kind of literary salon like what the Berry sisters have. I am certain it will be all the rage, and we shall end up having to learn to read Greek.'' She shook her head dolefully at the prospect. ''They intend to sponsor Miss Cassiopeia for a Season you know.''

''I suppose she will take,'' Mrs. Beetling said grudgingly. ''What with her aunt a patroness of Almack's and with a twenty-thousand-pound dowry.''

Lady Battford sighed at the nearly full glass on the table.

''What ever happened to that nice friend of Miss Montgomery's? That pretty girl and her brother?''

Her companion looked thoughtful. ''I don't know, really. I heard that there was some scandal up in London. Some havey-cavey business dealings, but I believe the whole matter was dropped.''

''I never thought that they were quite the thing anyway. I told Mr. Beetling just the other day that I thought they were cits from the start. Celia wanted to invite them to her ridotto, but I said she should not. Here is Louisa Montgomery.'' She indicated the doorway, where a footman was helping Cassiopeia with her aunt's wheeled chair.

''Do you know what I heard?'' Lady Battford said suddenly, putting her glass aside and leaning forward over the table. ''There is to be another wedding in the Montgomery family soon.''

''Cassiopeia and that Wellborne man? He did seem to

pay her particular attention . . .'' Mrs. Beetling lowered her voice conspiratorially.

"Louisa Montgomery and Lord Falk!"

"What?"

"Indeed, it is the most peculiar thing. Apparently he courted her years ago, but they fell out. Now they have decided to marry. And neither of them a day younger than eighty-five! It's quite the talk of Bath!"

Mrs. Beetling leaned back with an expression of satisfaction. "I knew it. I said from the first that she had her eye on him."

ABOUT THE AUTHOR

Catherine Blair lives in California. She is currently working on her next Zebra Regency romance, *A Family for Gillian,* which will be published in October 2001. Catherine loves to hear from readers and you may write to her c/o Zebra Books. Please include a self-addressed stamped envelope if you wish a response.